With a humourless laugh Angelos forced himself to accept the obvious... It had been amazing!

Deceitful she might be, but Chantal had also been a virgin—and the fact that he'd been her first lover had given him an incredible buzz.

Which meant that clearly he wasn't as modern in his attitudes as he liked to think.

She was here now, wasn't she?

The chemistry between them was amazing.

What was the problem?

She was here for a free holiday with a billionaire, so why not give her that holiday? And if it cost him a few dresses and the odd diamond necklace, so what?

They'd share incredible sex during the night, and during the day he'd arrange for her to spend as much time shopping as she could handle.

She was using him for money, so why shouldn't he use her in the bedroom?

Sarah Morgan trained as a nurse, and has since worked in a variety of health-related jobs. Married to a gorgeous businessman, who still makes her knees knock, she spends most of her time trying to keep up with their two little boys, but manages to sneak off occasionally to indulge her passion for writing romance. Sarah loves outdoor life, and is an enthusiastic skier and walker. Whatever she is doing, her head is always full of new characters, and she is addicted to happy endings.

Sarah also writes for Medical™ Romance!

BOUGHT:
THE GREEK'S
INNOCENT VIRGIN

BY
SARAH MORGAN

MILLS & BOON®
Pure reading pleasure

First published in Great Britain 2008
Harlequin Mills & Boon Limited,
Eton House, 18-24 Paradise Road, Richmond, Surrey TW9 1SR

© Sarah Morgan 2008

ISBN: 978 0 263 86434 2

Set in Times Roman 10 on 12 pt
01-0608-54758

Printed and bound in Spain
by Litografia Rosés, S.A., Barcelona

BOUGHT:
THE GREEK'S
INNOCENT VIRGIN

CHAPTER ONE

'I'VE FOUND HER, Angelos. And she's a goddess.'

Hearing the sound of his father's voice, Angelos Zouvelekis interrupted his conversation with the Greek ambassador to France and turned. 'Found who?' The fact that his father had made an effort to come tonight was a good sign. A few months ago he had been a broken man, unwilling to leave his isolated villa after his second painful divorce in six years.

'The perfect woman for you.' His father shook his head in disbelief, but the corners of his eyes crinkled as he smiled. 'Sometimes I wonder if you're really my son. This place is full of gorgeous, beautiful women and what do you do? You talk to boring men in suits. Where did I go wrong with you?'

Seeing the surprise in the ambassador's eyes, Angelos smoothly excused himself and drew his father to one side. 'For me, tonight is about business. I hold this ball every year. The purpose is to part the rich and famous from their money.'

'Business, business, business.' Visibly exasperated, his father raised his hands in despair. 'Does business keep you warm at night? Does it cook you dinner? Does it raise your children? *Always* with you it is business, Angelos, and already you are a billionaire! You have enough money! You don't need any more money! *What you need is a good woman!*'

Several heads turned in their direction, but Angelos simply

laughed. 'Tonight I'm not making money. I'm giving it away. And you're shocking everyone. Behave yourself,' he said mildly, 'or I'll tell Security to remove you from the building.' But it had been such a long time since his father had summoned sufficient energy to nag him about marriage that he felt nothing but relief. 'And I don't need you to find me a woman.'

'Why? Do you find one on your own? No, you don't. Not a proper one. You spend your time with women who would not make suitable wives.'

'That's why I pick them,' Angelos murmured, but his father frowned his disapproval, dismissing his comment with another wave of his hand.

'I know who you pick! The whole world knows who you pick, Angelos, because the stories are in every newspaper. One week it is a Savannah, the next it is a Gisella—never the same woman for more than a few weeks, and always they are thin, thin, thin.' His Greek accent thickening his words, Costas Zouvelekis made a disparaging noise. 'How can you be happy with a woman who doesn't enjoy her food? Does a woman like that cook for you? No. Does she enjoy life? No, of course not. How can a woman enjoy life when she is starving hungry? The women you pick have the legs and the hair, and they are like athletes in the bedroom, but would they care for your children? No. Would they—?'

'I don't need a woman to cook. I have staff for that purpose.' Angelos wondered briefly whether inviting his father to this particular function might have been a mistake after all. 'And I don't have any children for a woman to care for.'

His father gave a snort of exasperation. 'I know you don't, and I *want* you to have children. That is the point I am making! You are thirty-four years old and how many times have you been married? None. I am sixty-three and how many times have I been married? Three. It is time you started catching up, Angelos. Make me a grandfather!'

'Ariadne has already made you a grandfather twice.'

'That's different. She's my daughter and you are my son. I want to hold the sons of my son in my arms.'

'I'll get married when I find the right woman, not before.' Angelos drew his father onto the balcony that circled the ballroom and refrained from pointing out that his father's last two attempts at marriage had created emotional and financial devastation.

There was no way he was making that mistake.

'You won't find the right woman by dating the wrong ones! And what are we doing in Paris? Why can't you hold this ball in Athens? *What is wrong with Athens?*'

'The world is bigger than Greece.' Angelos suppressed a yawn as the conversation shifted onto another familiar topic. 'I conduct business all over the globe.'

'And I never understand why! Did I have to leave Greece to make my first million? No!' Costas peered into the ballroom. 'Where has she gone? I can't see her.'

Angelos raised his eyebrows in question. 'Who are you looking for?'

'The goddess with the body. She was perfect. And now she has disappeared. She was all eyes and curves and soft-looking. Now, *that* girl would make a good mother. I can imagine her with your children snuggled on her lap and a moussaka cooling on your table.'

Angelos glanced at his father with amusement. 'I suggest you don't tell her that. These days it is heresy to make that sort of comment to a woman. They invariably have rather different aspirations.'

'The women *you* pick have different aspirations.' His father's voice was fierce as he searched the room with his eyes. 'Believe me, this one was built to be a mother. If you don't want her, then I might be interested myself.'

All trace of amusement left him, and Angelos inhaled sharply.

'Not again!' *Didn't his father ever learn?* 'Promise me that this time you'll just take her to bed. *Don't* marry her,' he advised, taking a glass of orange juice from a passing waiter and swapping it for the glass of champagne in his father's hand.

'You only think about bed and sex, but I have more respect for women than that.'

'You need to develop a more cynical approach to the opposite sex,' Angelos advised. 'What respect did Tara show you when she left you after six months, taking with her enough money to keep her going for life?'

His father's knuckles whitened as he gripped the stem of the glass. 'We both made a mistake.'

Mistake? Angelos ground his teeth. He was sure that as far as Tara was concerned the marriage had been a resounding success. She was now an extremely rich young woman.

His father deflated before his eyes, his vulnerability exposed. 'She was very mixed up. She didn't know what she wanted.'

'She knew *exactly* what she wanted—' Angelos broke off, trapped between the option of upsetting his father still further by highlighting the ruthless efficiency of Tara's campaign, or of letting the subject drop and risking the possibility that, even after two such divorces, his trusting father *still* hadn't learned the lessons that needed to be learned.

Costas sighed. 'A relationship should be about love and caring.'

Angelos winced at this sentimental and dangerous observation and made a mental note to instruct his security team to screen all women showing the slightest interest in his father in order to protect him from further unscrupulous individuals. 'Didn't your last two marriages teach you anything about women?'

'Yes. They taught me that you can't trust a thin one.' Costas regained some of his spirit. 'They want to be size zero—but why is it called that? Because they are zero use to anyone! They are too thin and hungry to live the life a woman is supposed to live. Next time I marry she will be a proper shape.'

'After everything that has happened over the past six years, you *still* believe that love exists?'

His father's face fell. 'I was in love with your mother for forty years. Of course I believe that love exists.'

Cursing himself for his lack of tact, Angelos put a hand on his father's shoulder. 'You should stop trying to replace her,' he said roughly. 'What you had was rare.' So rare that he'd given up hope of finding it himself. And he wasn't willing to risk settling for anything less.

'I will find it again.'

Not before it had cost the family a fortune in divorce settlements and mental anguish

Frustrated by his father's misguided optimism about the female sex, Angelos ran a hand over the back of his neck. 'Stay single. It's less complicated.'

'I'm not staying single. I hate being single. It isn't natural for a man to be single. And you shouldn't be single, either.'

Seeing that his father was about to launch into another lecture in favour of the curvaceous woman, Angelos decided that the conversation had gone on long enough. 'You don't need to worry about me. I'm seeing a woman.' It wasn't the relationship that his father was hoping for, but he didn't need to know that.

His father scowled at him suspiciously. 'Is she a proper shape?'

'She is a perfect shape,' Angelos drawled, thinking of the A list Hollywood actress who had spent two *extremely* exciting nights in his bed the week before. Would he be seeing her again? Possibly. She had the legs and the hair and she was definitely an athlete in the bedroom. Was he interested in marrying her? Absolutely not. They would bore each other to death within a month, let alone a lifetime.

But hope was already lighting his father's eyes. 'And when will I meet her? You never introduce me to your girlfriends.'

With good reason. Introducing a woman to his father would deliver the exact message he was so careful never to send. 'When a woman is important to me, you will meet her,' Angelos said smoothly. 'And now I want to introduce you to Nicole. She's my Director of Public Affairs here in Paris, and she definitely loves food. I know you'll have plenty to say to one another.' He guided his father towards the reliable Nicole, made the necessary introductions, and then turned back to the ballroom to continue networking.

And stopped dead, his attention caught by the woman directly in front of him.

She walked as though she owned the place, with a gentle swing of her hips and a faint smile on her glossy mouth, as if something or someone had amused her. Her blonde hair was piled on her head and her vivid red dress provided a dazzling splash of colour amidst the predictable boring black. *She looked like an exotic rainforest bird let loose among a flock of crows.*

Instantly forgetting the Hollywood actress, Angelos watched her for a moment and then gave a slow, satisfied smile of his own. His father would be pleased on two counts, he thought, as he moved purposefully towards the unknown woman. Firstly because he was about to stop thinking about business and turn his attentions to the pursuit of pleasure, and secondly because the source of that pleasure definitely, very definitely, had curves.

Not that he required her to perform the various domestic functions that his father had listed. Despite his father's obvious concerns for him, he wasn't interested in a woman's capacity to cook, clean or raise his children. At this point in his life all he expected from a woman was entertainment, and she looked as though she'd been designed for exactly that purpose.

* * *

Smile, walk, smile, don't panic—

It was like being back in the school playground, with the bullies circling like gladiators while the malevolent crowd of girls pressed in, watching with sadistic fascination. Waiting for the kill.

The memory was so disturbingly vivid that feelings of terror and humiliation stirred to life, catching her unawares. No matter how many years passed, her past was always there, lurking inside her like dark, filthy slime.

She struggled to throw off all her old insecurities.

It was ridiculous to think of that here, now, when that part of her life had ended long ago.

This wasn't the playground, and she'd moved beyond that. The bullies might still be out there, but they couldn't see her any more. Her disguise was perfect.

Or was it?

She shouldn't have worn red. Red made her stand out like a beacon. And if she didn't eat something soon she was going to pass out.

Didn't anyone eat at these functions?

Wasn't anyone else starving hungry?

No wonder they were thin.

Wishing she'd never decided to test herself in this way, Chantal attempted to stroll casually across the room. *Confidence is everything*, she reminded herself. *Chin high, eyes up. Red is fine. They're only people. Don't let them intimidate you. They know nothing about you. From the outside you more or less look like them, and they can't see who you are on the inside.*

To distract herself, she played her usual game of make-believe. The game she'd invented as a means to survive in the lawless, ruthless environment she'd inhabited as a child. Her life had followed a pattern. A new playground, a new set of lies. A new layer of protection.

Who was she going to be this evening?

An heiress, maybe? Or possibly an actress?

A model?

No. Not a model. She would never be able to convince anyone that she was a model. She wasn't tall enough or thin enough.

She paused, still pondering her options. Nothing too complicated. Not that she was worried about being found out, because she would never see any of these people again.

Just for tonight, she could be anyone she wanted to be.

A penniless Italian *contessa* with lots of breeding and no money?

No. This was a charity ball. It wouldn't do to admit to having no money.

An heiress would be best.

An heiress wishing to remain incognito to avoid fortune hunters.

Yes. That was a good one.

Her excuse for not spending the money she didn't have would be that she didn't want to draw attention to herself.

The ballroom was amazing, with its high ceilings and glittering chandeliers. She had to remind herself not to stare at the paintings or the statues, and to adopt an expression of casual indifference—as though this was her world and such an exhibition of art and culture surrounded her on a daily basis.

As if—

'Champagne?' The question came from behind her and she turned swiftly, her eyes widening as she was confronted by a man so devilishly good-looking that every woman in the room was watching him longingly.

Her limbs weakened.

Arrogant, was the first word that came to mind.

Devastating, was the second.

His eyes glittered dark and he studied her with a disturbing degree of interest as he handed her a glass.

What was it about dinner jackets, she mused, that turned men into gods? Not that this man needed the assistance of well cut clothes to look good. He would have looked good in anything—or nothing. He was also the sort of man who wouldn't have looked twice at her in normal circumstances.

Chantal felt a sudden explosion of awareness engulf her body, and a deadly sexual warmth spread across her pelvis and down her limbs. He hadn't touched her. He hadn't even shaken her hand. And yet—

Dangerous was the word that finally caused her to take a defensive step backwards.

'I thought I knew everyone on the invitation list, but obviously I was wrong.' He spoke with the easy confidence that was the natural inheritance of the rich and powerful, his voice smooth and seductive, one dark eyebrow raised in anticipation of an introduction.

Still struggling to understand the reaction of her body, Chantal ignored the question in his eyes. She wasn't about to introduce herself—not least because she wasn't on the invitation list. Nor was she ever likely to be on the invitation list for an event like this.

She studied him for a moment, taking in the lean perfection of his bone structure and the lazy amusement in his eyes. He was looking at her in the way a man looked at a woman he was interested in taking to bed, and for a moment Chantal forgot to breathe.

Definitely dangerous.

The chemistry between them was so intense and so inexplicable that she felt flustered and hot.

Common sense told her that this was the time to make an elegant excuse and move on. She couldn't afford to indulge in a flirtation with anyone, because to draw that much attention to herself was to risk being exposed. 'Obviously you're a man who likes to be in control of his environment.'

'Am I?'

'If you're expecting to know everyone on the invitation list, then yes. That suggests a need to be in control, don't you think?'

'Or perhaps I'm just selective about who I spend time with.'

'Which means that you prefer the predictable to the possible. Knowing everyone surely limits the opportunity for surprises?'

His dark eyes gleamed with appreciation. 'I'm not easy to surprise. In my experience, the possible almost always turns out to be the probable. People are boringly predictable.' His mouth was a sensuous curve and she knew—*she just knew*—that this man would know everything there was to know about kissing a woman.

For a moment the mental image of his handsome dark head bending towards hers was so vivid that she couldn't formulate a reply, and his eyes drifted to her mouth, as if he were enjoying a similar fantasy.

'What? No argument? No desire to prove me wrong?' His gaze slid to the curved neckline of her dress and rested for a moment on her narrow waist. 'Tell me something about yourself that's likely to surprise me.'

Just about anything about her would have surprised him.

Her background.

Her true identity.

The fact that she wasn't supposed to be here.

'I'm starving,' she said truthfully, and he laughed with genuine amusement.

The sound turned heads in their direction, but he didn't seem to care. 'That's you at your most surprising?'

She glanced around her, her eyes resting on the impossibly slender frame of the nearest woman. 'It's pretty surprising to admit to liking food in this sort of company. I don't see a single woman here who is likely to be battling an addiction to chocolate truffles.'

'You don't see a single *real* woman. If you're hungry, then you must eat.' He lifted a hand and attracted the attention of a waiter with the natural confidence of someone used to being in control. She watched enviously, wishing she possessed even a fraction of his poise.

'I assumed the canapés were just for show.'

'You think their purpose is to test the self control of the guests?'

'If so, then I'm about to fail that test.' Smiling at the waiter, Chantal handed him her empty glass and piled several morsels on her napkin, resisting the temptation to snatch the entire trayful and put them in her handbag for later. 'Thank you. These look delicious.' The waiter bowed and moved away.

'So why are you hungry?' The man's eyes lingered on her hair. 'You haven't eaten all day because you were at the hairdresser's?'

She hadn't eaten all day because she'd worked a double shift serving food to other people. And because there was no point in wasting money on food when you knew a free meal was coming.

'Something like that.' Sliding a morsel of warm pastry into her mouth, Chantal struggled not to moan with delight as the texture and flavour exploded on her palate. 'These *are* delicious. Aren't you going to try one?'

His eyes were on her lips, and that simple connection was enough to stoke the flames that were licking around her pelvis.

They were in a crowded ballroom. So why did it feel as though it was just the two of them?

Flustered, she realised that she really, really needed to leave— but at that moment he helped himself to a canapé from her napkin, and the gesture was strangely intimate. Chantal was wondering how eating could be intimate when he smiled at her, and that smile was so irresistibly sexy that she couldn't do anything except smile back.

'You're right, they *are* delicious.' He lifted his hand and gently brushed a crumb from the corner of her mouth. 'So far all I know about you is that you like food and that you don't spend all day obsessing about your figure. Are you going to give me any more clues about yourself?'

'Why?'

'I'd like an introduction.'

She felt her heart skip and jump. 'If I tell you my name then you'll have to tell me *your* name, and it's much more fun if we remain strangers.'

He was silent for a moment. 'You don't know my name?'

'Of course not.'

The faint gleam in his eyes told her that this wasn't the answer he'd expected. 'All right,' he drawled softly, 'no names. So, how would you describe yourself?'

A liar, a cheat and a fraud?

'A person's perception of themselves is almost always at odds with how others perceive them,' Chantal murmured, choosing to be intentionally vague. 'But I like to think of myself as—adaptable.'

'You're not going to tell me who you really are?'

She didn't want to think about who she really was. Suppressing a shudder, Chantal gave what she hoped was a mysterious smile. 'Does it matter? Perhaps I'm a princess? Or maybe I'm the CEO of a corporation? Or an heiress determined to hide her identity?'

'All of those people were included on the invitation list. So which are you? Princess, heiress or CEO?' His tone was dry, but his eyes were sharp and assessing and Chantal knew that she ought to end the conversation and move on immediately. This man's intelligence was not in dispute, and it wouldn't take him long to work out that there was something about her that didn't ring true.

It didn't matter how much she struggled to bury it, the darkness of her past was always there—a constant reminder that all this was all a pretence.

'I'm a woman. The sort of woman who prefers not to be

stereotyped. I like to think that our horizons can be as broad as we want them to be.'

'You think I stereotype women?'

'I'm sure you do it all the time. Everyone does.' Trying to look as though she belonged in this environment, Chantal pretended to smile a greeting at someone across the room. Unfortunately for her, the man in question chose that moment to look at her and smile back. Flustered, she turned away. *It was definitely time to leave.* 'I don't like labels. I prefer to be just—me.'

Now that they'd finished the canapés, the man lifted two more glasses of champagne from the tray of a passing waiter and handed her one. 'The mere fact that you are here tells me a great deal about you.'

'Really?' Engulfed by a wave of horror at the thought of him knowing even the slightest bit about her, Chantal took a large mouthful of champagne.

'Yes.' His eyes narrowed thoughtfully as they rested on her face. 'Tickets to this event are highly sought after and difficult to obtain. In order to have been among the lucky few, you have to be seriously wealthy.'

Chantal thought of the dingy room she'd left a few hours earlier. The landlord had increased the rent, and in two weeks' time she'd be homeless.

The only jobs that paid decently she wasn't prepared to do.

'The concept of wealth means different things to different people,' she murmured, curling her fingers around the stem of the glass. 'Is it money or is it good health? Or perhaps a warm, loving family? To consider wealth to be the exclusive privilege of those with money is to risk missing out on a full life, don't you agree?'

There was a cynical tone to his laugh. 'If you truly believe that, then you're an unusual woman. Most members of your sex think that money is the *only* route to a full life.'

People were openly staring at them and Chantal felt a flicker of panic. Could they see through the red dress and the make-up? She felt as though she had the word 'impostor' stamped on her forehead in large letters. Her hand shaking, she took another mouthful of champagne. 'There you go again—stereotyping. Clearly you regard women as a homogonous breed, endowed with identical characteristics.'

'Most of the women I meet *are* a homogonous breed,' he said dryly, and for a moment she forgot about the people watching them and looked at him curiously, wondering what events in his life had triggered that remark.

He was handsome, yes, but there was also a hardness to him. An outer shell that she guessed wouldn't be easily penetrated. Perhaps she recognised it because she'd developed the same shell herself.

'Maybe you're moving in the wrong circles. Or perhaps there's something about you that attracts a particular type of woman.'

'That would be my wallet.' His smile was impossibly sexy, and Chantal was captivated by the unexpected glimpse of humour that lay beneath his sophisticated exterior.

In fact she was enjoying the conversation so much that she just couldn't quite bring herself to end it, even though she knew she should. Talking to him had restored her much needed confidence. He made her feel beautiful, and the attraction between them was something she'd never encountered before. *Powerful, intoxicating....*

'So I assume that's why people are staring at us,' she said lightly. 'They're wondering whether I'm about to put my hand in your pocket and rob you.'

Without warning he lifted a hand and gently trailed ran his finger over the curve of his jaw, a thoughtful look in his eyes. 'The men are staring because you're the most beautiful woman in the room.'

The unexpected compliment took her breath away. 'Really?'

She struggled to keep her tone light. 'So why aren't they all queuing up to drag me onto the dance floor?'

'Because you're with me.' His tone was casual, but there was a steely undertone that instantly dismissed the competition.

Possessive, she thought to herself, trying desperately to ignore the thrill of excitement that buzzed through her body like an electric current.

He was the most confident, self assured man she'd ever met, and he was way out of her league. She was playing a dangerous, dangerous game by lingering, and she knew that she ought to walk away before the situation grew more complicated.

Before her lies exploded in her face.

But Chantal couldn't move. She felt more alive then she'd ever felt before. 'That doesn't explain why the women are glaring at me.'

The gleam in his eyes suggested that he considered her question ridiculously naive. 'The women are glaring because they're nervous about their men. You are *serious* competition. And they're trying to work out which designer is responsible for your incredible dress.'

Chantal wasn't sure whether it was his words or the seductive stroke of his fingers that caused the sudden rush of heat through her body.

'My dress is a one off, designed specifically for me,' she said truthfully. 'And I have a feeling that the women are glaring at me because I'm talking to you.' And she couldn't blame them for that. He was a man who would incite jealousy wherever he went.

He was breathtakingly gorgeous and she wondered briefly about his nationality. He wasn't French and didn't look English. But his English was perfect. The product of a first-class education.

At that unsettling thought, her insecurities sprang to life again and she reminded herself that for now, at least, he was with *her*.

Yes, they were surrounded by stick-thin, stunning model types, but *she* was the one he was smiling at.

And she didn't even bother trying to subdue the little flicker of triumph that accompanied *that* realisation.

Perhaps it had been worth coming after all, just to experience this one perfect moment.

In a room full of the very cream of society, he'd singled her out.

Knowing that, wasn't it time she left her insecurities in the past?

'They're not looking at me.' His hand fell to his side and there was a cynical gleam in his eyes. 'Or if they are then they're not seeing me. They're seeing my wallet. When it comes to dress size they want to see one zero, but when it comes to a man's wallet they're rather more ambitious.'

Chantal laughed, and refrained from pointing out that he could be penniless and women would still stare. 'If you're so rich that women can't see past your wallet, then there's an obvious solution.' Her eyes twinkling, she stood on tiptoe and spoke softly in his ear, 'Give away all your money.'

His head turned fractionally, so that his lips almost brushed her cheek. 'You think I should do that?'

He smelt amazing, Chantal thought dizzily, resting a hand on his shoulder to steady herself. 'It would stop women stereotyping you as a rich, available man.'

'How do you know I'm available?'

Feeling distinctly light-headed, Chantal stepped away slightly, deciding regretfully that it really was time to move on from this conversation and this man. *Before she forgot who she really was.* 'Because if you weren't, some extremely jealous woman would have stabbed me in the back with her cutlery by now.'

His eyes were on her mouth. 'So your advice is to give away my money?'

'Absolutely. Only then can you be sure of a woman's motives.'

The musicians started to play the seductive, powerful notes of a tango, and Chantal closed her eyes for a moment, wishing they hadn't chosen that particular moment to perform that number.

It reminded her of Buenos Aires.

She'd spent two months travelling around Argentina, and she loved South American music.

The rhythm was so familiar that her body swayed instinctively, and the next moment the glass was removed from her hand and she felt her mysterious companion slide a hand around her back and pull her close. So close that, had the dance not been a tango, their contact would have drawn comment.

Her eyes opened. 'What are you doing?'

'Dancing. With you.'

'You didn't ask me.'

'I never ask a question when I already know the answer. It wastes time.'

'Arrogant,' she murmured, and he gave a slow smile.

'Self-aware.'

'Over-confident.' Laughing, she tilted her head to look at him. 'I might have said no.' She could feel the warmth of his hand on the bare skin at the base of her spine and the contact sent spirals of heat coursing through her body.

'You wouldn't have said no.'

And he was absolutely right.

There was no way she would have been able to say no to this man.

The throbbing, sexy music coiled itself around them and Chantal was breathlessly conscious of the strength and power of his body pressed against hers.

He clasped her hand in his and drew her nearer still, until it felt as though there wasn't a single part of her that wasn't touching him. The music washed over them and he moved in response to that intoxicating rhythm, using subtle changes in pressure to lead her around the dance floor.

She was so aware of him that she couldn't breathe. He was in her personal space and she felt suffocated and seduced at the same time, intoxicated and drugged by the powerful chemistry that had erupted between them from the first moment they'd met.

What they were doing ceased to feel like dancing. It was—

An exploration of sexuality?

Her body slid over his, his leg following her leg, his hands on her hips. He moved with a confidence and innate sensuality that left her in no doubt that this man would be an incredible lover.

For some lucky woman.

And that woman would never be someone like her.

But for now—just for now—he was hers. And she was going to make the most of the moment.

They danced chest to chest, eyes locked, breath mingling, the heat and their chemistry turning the dance into something close to a primal mating ritual.

Chantal ceased to register the other people on the dance floor and suddenly there was just the two of them, their bodies moving together in perfect understanding as they executed something far deeper and more complex than a few dance steps. It was erotic, passionate and deeply intimate. They'd never met before this evening, and yet instinctively she knew what he wanted from her and moved in response to his demands.

Her senses were heightened and she was lost in the music and the moment as they danced with fluency and sensuality. One moment they were chest to chest and she could feel the steady thump of his heartbeat against hers, and then he would turn her and she could feel the seductive slide of his hands over her hips as he moved her body in a dance that only just bordered on the socially acceptable. The movement of his leg drew the silk of her dress up her own leg, and the warmth of his breath against her neck made her shiver. How was it possible to be hot and cold at the same time?

How was it possible to feel this way about a man she'd never met before and wouldn't ever meet again?

Perhaps that was why, she mused, gasping slightly as he tipped her slightly off balance, forcing her to lean into his body. Because she would never see him again, she could let go and enjoy herself.

For tonight, she was this man's dance partner.

And dancing with him was shameful, sinful and like nothing she'd ever experienced before.

Her mind and body moved into a different place altogether and when the music finally shifted to a different rhythm it took her a moment to register her surroundings and return to reality.

They stared at each other for an endless moment, and then he released her and stepped away from her.

There was a strange light in his dark eyes as he studied her.

'I'll fetch us both a drink.' His tone was noticeably cooler than it had been before they'd danced.

He strode off and she blinked several times, disorientated by the sudden change in his attitude. A moment ago they'd been in another world, just the two of them, and now—

She took a few deep breaths, trying to settle the intense reaction of her body. He seemed angry—but why would he be angry?

It had been his choice to dance, not hers.

And she hadn't trodden on his toes or fallen on the floor.

Wondering what she'd done to bring about such a change in him, she was about to melt into the background when a woman approached her.

'I'm Marianna Killington-Forbes.' She spoke in a lazy English upper-class accent, and the smile that touched her mouth went nowhere near her eyes. 'You look very familiar. Have we met?'

Oh, yes, they'd met.

Chantal's legs started to shake as her disguise fell away. She felt naked and exposed, her past no longer safely concealed but rising in front of her like some vile, malevolent demon. She was going to die of embarrassment and humiliation. Right now. Right here. 'I—'

'She doesn't speak much English, Marianna. I told her to stay with me and not wander off, but we were separated in the crowd.' The heavily accented voice came from directly behind her, and Chantal turned to find a man by her side. She guessed him to be in his seventies, but he was still ridiculously handsome and his eyes were kind as he smiled down at her. He said something to her in a language that she didn't understand and then took her freezing cold hand in his, tucking it firmly into the bend of his arm as he drew her close. 'Marianna?' His eyes lost some of their warmth as he looked at her tormentor. 'Is there something that you wish to say? I can try and translate, if you would like?'

The woman's mouth tightened. 'She didn't seem to be having any problems communicating with Angelos.'

The man smiled. 'As you no doubt noticed, they use an entirely different method of communication.'

Jealousy flashed in the other woman's eyes and she turned her attention back to Chantal. 'Well, I wish you luck with your relationship. The ability not to converse could stand you in good stead, given that Angelos never expects conversation from his women anyway.'

Still frozen with horror that Marianna had recognised her face, Chantal watched with relief as the other woman stalked away, apparently unable to recall her name or exactly how she knew her.

'You're shaking.' The man's voice was soft, and Chantal clung to his arm, struggling to pull herself together. Desperately hoping that her dance partner wasn't going to choose that moment to reappear, she took several deep breaths.

'Do you think—could you just stay with me for a minute?' Her voice cracked. 'I don't want to be left on my own just now.'

'You are not on your own.' His hand covered hers, and she felt the warmth of his fingers thaw the chill in her bones.

'Thank you,' she whispered, so pathetically grateful for his intervention that she almost hugged him on the spot. 'I don't know why you did that, but I'll never forget it. You've been so, so kind. How did you know I needed rescuing?'

'When she walked up to you, your face turned white. I thought you were going to faint. You don't like her, no?'

'Well, I—'

'Don't be embarrassed. I don't like her either,' the man said firmly. 'I never could stand that woman. I wonder why she was invited.'

Chantal thought back to the misery of her schooldays. 'Her daddy is very rich.'

'Really? He clearly didn't spend his money feeding his family.' The man made a disparaging noise. 'To look at her you'd think she was starved from birth. Her bones should be classified as a lethal weapon. If you bumped into her, you'd be bruised all over.'

Despite her insecurities, Chantal couldn't help laughing. He was not only kind, he was also funny. She glanced at him curiously, thinking that he reminded her of someone. 'I'd better leave—' She started to move, but he tightened his grip on her arm.

'If you leave,' he said softly, 'then they'll think they've won. Is that what you want?'

She stilled, wondering how he knew what she was feeling. 'Everyone is staring at me—'

'So smile,' the man instructed calmly. 'Lift your chin and smile. You have as much right to be here as the rest of them.' Without giving her the chance to argue, he led her to two vacant chairs. 'Sit for a moment and keep a lonely old man company. I hate these things. I always feel out of place.'

'That can't possibly be true. You look as confident as anyone here.'

'But appearances can be deceptive, can't they?' His gentle comment made it clear that he was aware of how uncomfortable and insecure she felt.

His unusual insight probably should have worried her, but it didn't. All she felt was the most profound gratitude. Not only had he rescued her from a potentially embarrassing situation, he was now pretending that her fears and insecurities were nothing out of the ordinary.

'Why are you being so kind to me?'

'I'm not being kind. I hate these events. You can't blame me for enjoying myself with the best-looking woman in the room.'

She wished her hands would stop shaking. 'If you hate them, why did you come?'

'To please my son. He is worried that I haven't been getting out enough lately.'

'In that case he won't want to see you wasting your time with me.' And she should be leaving. Before Marianna remembered who she was.

'That dance—' The man glanced towards her, the corners of his eyes crinkling. 'It was like watching one person. The rhythm was perfect, the chemistry between the two of you— Only lovers can dance the Argentine tango like that.'

Lovers?

Chantal opened her mouth to tell him that they hadn't even exchanged names, but then decided that it would be embarrassing to admit that she'd danced like that with a total stranger.

What had Marianne called him? Angelos?

So she'd been right about one thing; *he definitely wasn't English.*

What would it be like, she mused dreamily, *to be loved by a man like that?*

'And even now you can't stop thinking about him, can you?' The man sounded pleased. 'You share something deep. He cares. I can see with my own eyes. The way he looked at you. The way you looked at him. The way you moved together, as if there was no one else in the room. The body says more than words. I can see from watching you that your relationship is serious.'

His observation shocked her out of her dreams. 'Oh. Well, no, it isn't exactly—'

'You don't have to be secretive with me. I may be old enough to be your father, but that doesn't mean I've forgotten what it's like to be in love. I want to know how you felt the first time you saw him. Tell me!'

Chantal hesitated and then smiled, drawn by the kindness in his eyes. It was strange, she mused. She didn't make friends easily, and yet after only five minutes in his company she would have died for this man. 'I thought he was amazing,' she said honestly. 'He was charming, clever and surprisingly easy to talk to.'

'And sexy?'

'Oh, yes. Incredible.' She lowered her voice, afraid that the people around them might overhear. 'I've never been so attracted to anyone in my life before.'

The man nodded with satisfaction. 'I knew it. And you're crazy about him, aren't you?'

'Well—' Chantal gave a helpless shrug. 'Yes. But we haven't exactly known each other for—'

'It's either right or it's wrong! All these long engagements— all nonsense. If a man and woman are right together, they're right straight away—not in six months or six years.'

Slightly disturbed by that comment, Chantal thought for a moment. *Right together?* Hardly. If he was as rich as she suspected, then she couldn't think of two people less suited.

She would never be comfortable in his world. And he wouldn't want her in his.

If he knew who she was then he'd join the crowd at the edge of the playground.

Dismissing that thought, she glanced at the man next to her. He really did remind her of someone. 'So, if you're such an expert on body language, why do you think he looked so angry?' She wondered why she was asking the advice of a total stranger. But he didn't feel like a stranger, and talking to him seemed like the most natural thing in the world.

'That's easy enough to answer. A man never likes to admit that he's well and truly fallen for a woman. I was the same when I met my wife. I struggled for weeks. Loving a woman makes a man vulnerable, and a strong man doesn't like to be vulnerable. I resisted her.'

'So what did your wife do to win you over?'

'She did what women always do when they want something. Talk, talk, talk until a man's resistance is ground into the dust.'

Chantal laughed. 'Are you still together?'

'We had forty years.' The man's smile faded. 'She died fifteen years ago and I've never met anyone else to touch her. But I haven't given up trying. And I can still remember how it feels to move around a dance floor.'

Moved by the emotion in his voice, Chantal stood up impulsively and held out her hands. 'Show me.' She angled her head and listened to the music. 'It's a waltz. Do you waltz?'

He laughed with delight. 'You want me to waltz with you?'

'Why is that funny?'

'I'm seventy three.'

'There's no man in the room I'd rather dance with.'

'Then you are a brave woman, because Angelos is an extremely possessive man. He would *not* be amused if I took you onto the dance floor. But I can see now why you've succeeded where so many have failed. I'm sure it's that wonderful spirit of yours that has made you different from all the others.'

'All the others?' Chantal frowned. 'All what others?'

'All the other women who have aspired to be where you are tonight. By his side. In his heart.' The man's eyes misted and Chantal felt her stomach lurch.

'You know him well?' Who exactly was this man? Desperately she tried to rerun the conversation. *Exactly what had she said?* 'You didn't mention that you knew him well.'

'If I'd done that you might not have talked so freely, and that would have been a pity. It was a most illuminating conversation.' The older man was still smiling, and at that moment Chantal saw her dance partner approach, the expression on his handsome face dark and forbidding.

He stopped in front of them, broad shouldered and powerful, an ominous frown touching his dark brows as he saw their clasped hands.

Chantal instantly withdrew her hands, her heart starting to thud. *Why was he looking at her like that?* The man she was sitting with was clearly a man of mature years. What possible reason was there for the shimmering anger she saw in the eyes of her handsome dance partner?

He couldn't possibly be jealous. That would be too ridiculous for words.

She didn't know what to say, so she just sat holding her breath, waiting for him to speak.

An expression of grim disapproval settled on his face as he glanced between the two of them and finally, after what seemed like an age, straightened his shoulders and spoke.

'I see you've met my father.'

CHAPTER TWO

CHANTAL served the group of tourists seated at the table and then sank into a chair at an adjacent table, staring blankly at an empty coffee cup.

It didn't matter how much time passed, she still felt horribly, miserably embarrassed. And sad. Really, really sad. As if she'd lost something special that she'd never be able to get back.

What was the matter with her?

Two weeks had passed since the ball. *Two weeks since she'd gate-crashed the most prestigious social event of the year—*

Why couldn't she just forget it and move on?

Why couldn't she just forget *him*?

Without thinking, she slipped a hand into the pocket of her skirt and touched the piece of torn newspaper she'd been carrying around for the past two weeks. She'd touched and stared at the picture so many times that it was crumpled and thin, and in immediate danger of falling apart. Now she wished that she'd bought a hundred copies of the newspaper and stored them safely, so that when she was old and grey she could remind herself of that one perfect night.

That one perfect man.

The memory of that dance still made her nerve-endings tingle. The chemistry that had sizzled between them had been the most exciting, astonishing experience of her life. Even now, as she remembered the seductive, intoxicating feel of his body against hers, her heart-rate increased.

But it hadn't just been the chemistry that had kept her by his side long after she should have made her escape. She'd *liked* him. She'd liked his sharp observations, his intelligence and his dry sense of humour.

Angelos Zouvelekis.

Thanks to the article in her pocket, she now knew exactly who he was.

Billionaire and philanthropist. *Greek* billionaire and philanthropist.

Of course. Greek. The clues had all been there, if she'd only looked for them. His hair was the deep, glossy black of a Kalamata olive and his bronzed skin hinted at a life spent bathed in the warmth of the Mediterranean sun.

She'd fallen for a Greek billionaire as well known for his bachelor status as for his phenomenal business success.

And, for her, the fairy tale ended there—because she couldn't have picked a more unsuitable man if she'd tried.

Tears stung her eyes and she blinked rapidly. *Ironic, really,* she thought to herself. Every other woman would have considered Angelos Zouvelekis to be the most suitable man on the planet. Every other woman would have known immediately who he was.

Not her. She hadn't had a clue. If she had, maybe she would have walked away sooner.

Found a different man to fall in love with.

Oh, for goodness' sake! She sucked in a breath, impatient with herself for thinking that way. No one fell in love that easily! It just didn't happen. What she was feeling wasn't love. It was just—just—

Rubbing a hand over her face, she struggled to pull herself together.

She didn't actually understand what it was that she was

feeling, but she wished it would stop because it was pulling her down. And anyway, what she felt about him was irrelevant, because he'd made it perfectly clear what he'd thought of her.

He'd been so, so angry.

Somehow—and she'd never actually found out how—he'd obviously discovered that she hadn't been invited to the ball.

Chantal covered her face with her hands and shook her head, trying to erase the hideously embarrassing memory. Just remembering his hard, icy tone made her want to sink through the floor.

What had he called her? Greedy, unscrupulous and dishonest.

And perhaps she'd deserved it. After all, it *had* been dishonest to use a ticket that wasn't hers.

To call her greedy and unscrupulous was a bit over the top, but, given the outrageous price of the tickets, she could see how he might have thought that about her.

And to make matters worse there had been that incredibly sticky moment when his father had expressed his undiluted joy that his son was finally in a loving relationship.

Remembering the look of thunderous incredulity that had transformed Angelos's features from handsome to intimidating, Chantal slid lower in her seat.

That had been the biggest mistake of all: voicing her dreams and fantasies to the elderly man who had helped her so much. But she'd adored him on sight, and he'd been so kind to her. So approachable and sympathetic. Almost a father figure, although she didn't really know what one of those looked like. As far as she was concerned, the species was extinct.

Perhaps that was why she'd been so drawn to him.

Angelos's father.

She gave a whimper of disbelief and regret. Of all the men in the room, why had she chosen *him* as a sounding board for her fantasies?

Telling herself firmly that it was in the past, and she needed to forget it, Chantal straightened her shoulders and tried to think positively about the future.

Obviously she couldn't stay in Paris. She needed to travel to somewhere remote. A place where there was absolutely no chance of bumping into one very angry Greek male. The Amazon, maybe? Or the Himalayas? Even a man with a global business wasn't likely to have an office in Nepal, was he?

She sat for a moment, trying to stir up some enthusiasm for her next step.

It was exciting to be able to travel anywhere and be anyone. She was lucky to be free to make the decisions she wanted to make. How many other people had absolutely no ties? Most people had jobs to restrict their movements, or families to think of. She had no such restrictions.

She had no family to answer to. No one who cared what she did. She could move continents tomorrow without having to ask anyone's permission, and she could be anyone she wanted to be.

Chantal waited for the usual buzz of excitement that came from the prospect of reinventing herself yet again, but nothing happened. Instead of the thrill of adventure, her mood was totally flat.

She felt as though she'd lost something and she didn't understand why she would feel that way.

What had she lost?

'Chantal!' The café owner's voice cut through the embarrassing memories like a sharp knife. 'I am not paying you to rest! We have customers. Get on your feet and serve them! This is your last warning.'

Chantal sprang to her feet, realising with another spurt of embarrassment that she'd sat down at the table she was supposed to be cleaning.

Her cheeks pink, she quickly gathered up the empty cup and two glasses and hurried into the kitchen.

'More time working and less time dreaming, or I'll be looking for a new waitress.' The small, rotund little Frenchman gave an unpleasant smile, openly staring at the thrust of her breasts under her white blouse. 'Unless you want to apply for a different role.'

Chantal lifted her eyes to his, his comment triggering a response so violent that it shocked her. It took her a moment to find her voice. 'Look for a new waitress,' she said hoarsely. 'I resign.' And, just to reinforce that decision, she removed the ridiculous little apron that she'd been forced to wear over the vestigial black skirt and white blouse.

The café owner thought that it attracted customers. And it did. But they were almost always the type of customer she would have chosen to avoid.

Vile self-loathing curled inside her and she thrust the apron into his hands, not even bothering to ask for the money he owed her.

She didn't care about the money.

She just wanted to get away. The truth was that Chantal, waitress, had never really worked for her. Neither had Chantal, chambermaid, or Chantal, barmaid.

The darkness of her past pressed in on her and she hurried towards the door, desperately needing to be outside in the warm Paris sunshine.

The café owner was subjecting her to a tirade of fluent French, but Chantal ignored him and virtually ran out of the door.

She'd move on. Travel somewhere exotic where she knew no one.

Maybe Egypt would be exciting. She could see the pyramids and swim in the Red Sea—

Calming down slightly, she left the café without glancing back and started to walk along the wide boulevard that led towards the Eiffel Tower. The trees were in full leaf, and the fountains bubbled and gushed, the sound soothing and cooling in the warm air.

It was lunchtime, and tourists mingled with elegantly dressed

Parisian mothers taking their toddlers for a stroll. A little blonde girl tripped and fell, and instantly her mother was by her side, gathering her into her arms for a hug.

Just for an instant Chantal watched, and then she put her head down and hurried on, ignoring the faint stab of envy that tore at her insides.

She was twenty-four; far too old to be envying a child her mother.

She quickened her pace, dodging a group of teenagers who were gliding in circles on rollerblades. They mocked each other and laughed, their effortless camaraderie making her feel even more wistful.

None of them looked displaced or insecure.

They all belonged.

Above her the Eiffel Tower rose high, but Chantal didn't spare it a glance. In the two months she'd spent in Paris she hadn't once joined the throngs who jostled with each other in long queues for a chance to reach the top. She'd avoided the standard tourist traps and opted instead to discover the hidden Paris.

But now it was time to move on.

Not thinking or caring about her destination, she just walked, determined to enjoy her last moments in a city she'd grown to love.

Eventually she reached the river Seine, and she paused for a moment on the embankment, watching the way the sun glinted on the water. Behind her cars roared past, weaving in and out of lanes in an alarmingly random fashion. Horns blared, and drivers shook their fists and yelled abuse at each other through open windows.

It was a typical day in Paris.

She crossed the river and made her way up to the Rue du Faubourg Saint-Honoré with its designer shops. This area was the heart of Paris design and fashion; Chanel, Lanvin, Yves St Laurent, Versace—they were all here. She paused outside a window, her attention caught by a dress on display, her brain automatically memorising the cut and the line.

Why were people prepared to pay such an indecent sum of money for something so simple? she mused. A length of fabric and a reel of cotton thread could produce the same for a fraction of the amount.

The dress she'd made for the ball had been a huge success, and no one had seemed to recognise it as an old piece of discarded curtain lining.

The low growl of a powerful engine broke her concentration, and she glanced behind her as a shiny black Lamborghini jerked to a halt in the road.

Chantal felt her heart skitter, and slowly the world around her faded into the background. She was oblivious to the fact that several other women had turned to stare and equally oblivious to the cacophony of car horns as other drivers registered their protest.

She knew that car.

She'd seen it two weeks before—at the ball she hadn't been invited to.

It belonged to the man that she hadn't been supposed to dance with.

The son of the man she wished she'd never talked to.

His attention caught by the gleaming blonde hair and long, long legs of the woman staring into the shop window, Angelos Zouvelekis slammed his foot on the brake and brought the car to an abrupt halt.

Ignoring the sudden swivel of heads that followed his action, he stared hard at the woman.

Was it her?

Had he finally found her, or was it wishful thinking on his part?

She looked different. Wondering if he'd made a mistake,

Angelos narrowed his eyes and imagined this woman with her hair piled on top of her head and her arms and shoulders revealed by the clever cut of her couture dress.

And then her eyes met his, and all doubt faded. Even from this distance he caught a flash of sapphire-blue—the same unusual colour that had caught his attention that fateful night at the ball.

Her eyes were unforgettable.

Finally he'd found her. And where else but shopping in one of the most expensive districts of Paris?

It should have been the first place he'd instructed his security team to look, Angelos thought cynically, wondering which deluded fool had provided the money she was clearly about to spend.

The fact that he'd been compelled to search for her at all made the anger explode inside him and he switched off the engine and sprang from the car, as indifferent to the 'No Parking' signs as he was to the gaping audience of admiring women who were now watching his movements with lustful interest.

At that precise moment he wasn't interested in any woman except the one who was staring at him, and he almost laughed as he saw the shock in her eyes.

It didn't surprise him that she was shocked to see him, given the way they'd parted company.

He was shocked, too. In normal circumstances he went out of his way to avoid women like her. If anyone had told him a month ago that he would have used all his contacts to track down someone whose behaviour appalled and disgusted him, he would have laughed.

But here he was, about to make her day. Thanks to a twist of fate, he was about to give her all she'd dreamed of and more.

As he walked purposefully towards her he consoled himself with the knowledge that although she had won the first round, the second, third and fourth were going to be his.

She was also about to discover the truth behind that famous saying *Be careful what you wish for...*

This woman had made her wishes perfectly clear, but he was absolutely sure that by the time he'd finished with her she would be wishing she'd targeted a man less able to defend himself.

Angelos ground his teeth, furious and frustrated at the position he now found himself in. She was obviously the sort of woman who devoted her life to leeching from those better off than her. A woman with no scruples and no morals. She was the lowest of the low, and the knowledge that he'd been well and truly manipulated for the first time in his life did nothing for his temper.

If there was one word he would never have applied to himself, it was *gullible*.

He looked straight at her, and was instantly gripped by a spasm of lust so powerful that his brain momentarily ceased to function.

She was all woman.

From the tumbling blonde hair to the generous swell of her breasts and the soft curve of her narrow waist, she was entirely and uncontrovertibly feminine.

Over the past two weeks he'd been so furiously angry with her that he'd forgotten how incredibly beautiful she was. Her assets would not have been valued by any of the glossy magazines—her shape was too feminine for that—but she was a woman that any red-blooded male would fantasise about taking to bed.

Appalled at himself, Angelos dragged his gaze away from her and tried to refocus his mind.

It had been a long two weeks, he reminded himself as he searched for a logical explanation for his unwelcome and wholly inappropriate reaction to her. An extremely long two weeks.

Back in control, he risked another glance at her. This time he thought he saw guilt in her eyes and had to remind himself that guilt was connected to conscience, and this woman wasn't familiar with either word.

'Isabelle.' He was unable to keep the contempt out of his voice and for a moment she just stared at him, wide eyed, her expression faintly puzzled.

Then she spoke, and her voice was husky and feminine. 'Who is Isabelle?'

The denial on her part was entirely predictable, but all the same temper exploded inside him. 'We are no longer playing "Guess the Identity".'

'But I'm not—'

'Don't!' Driven to the limits of his self control, he growled the warning and she backed away a few steps.

As well she might, Angelos thought grimly, *after the stunt she'd pulled.*

'Get in the car.' He was too angry to bother with pleasantries, and he saw a flicker of panic in her eyes.

'You've obviously mistaken me for someone else.'

He reached into his pocket and removed the evidence. 'There's no mistake. Next time you're trying to remain incognito, *don't* drop your ticket.'

She stared at the ticket in his hand, and it was clear that she didn't know what to say.

'Now I understand why you were so reluctant to introduce yourself.' He watched the various emotions flicker across her eyes. Consternation, confusion—*fear*? 'So now we've cleared up the sticky subject of your identity, let's go.'

She was still looking at the ticket. 'Go where?'

'With me. This is your lucky day.' He wondered whether it was possible for words to actually choke a man. 'You've hit the jackpot.'

Her gaze shifted from the ticket to his face. 'I honestly don't know what you're talking about.'

So, not only had she won this round, but she intended to make him suffer by rubbing it in.

He was so livid that had he been a lion he would have savaged her on the spot and left her body for the hyenas.

As it was, the desire to walk away was so powerful that he actually stepped back from her. Then a vision of his father flew into his head and he reminded himself of the reason he was standing here now.

Cursing softly, he ran a hand over the back of his neck, wondering if there had been any change in his father's condition.

Reminding himself that the sooner this was sorted, the sooner he could return to Greece and monitor his father's progress in person, Angelos stood his ground. 'Amazing though it seems, I'm about to further the acquaintance that you saw fit to initiate.' Furious at finding himself manipulated by a set of circumstances that were now far beyond his control, he tightened his jaw. 'Get in the car.'

'I really need to tell you something—' she sounded young, and just a little bit desperate, but he was too angry to feel sympathy.

He knew from personal experience that youth and greed existed happily together. Thanks in part to the numerous glossy magazines that made their profit from fuelling envy, there were plenty of people who wanted maximum lifestyle for minimum effort.

'I'm not interested in anything you have to say. This time *I'm* doing the talking, and I don't want an audience.'

She didn't move, and the crowd of people behind her seemed to have grown larger. 'I don't see what there is to talk about.'

'You'll find out soon enough. Unlike you, I prefer to keep my personal business personal. Let's go.' *Before someone recognised him and took a photograph that would appear in tomorrow's newspapers.* 'My hotel isn't far from here.'

'Your *hotel*?' Her expression grew suddenly frosty, as if he'd delivered the worst insult possible. 'Pick another girl, Mr Zouvelekis. I'm not the sort of woman who likes to become intimately acquainted with the inside of a man's hotel room—even less so when that man is a stranger.'

Her prim, dignified rejection was so at odds with what he already knew about her character that he didn't know whether to laugh or punch something.

'A stranger?' He failed to keep the disdain out of his voice. 'I'm the same stranger that you danced with, and we both know where that dance would have led. If you hadn't shown your true colours so early in the evening, we would have ended the night naked in my hotel room.'

Her lips parted in murmured denial, but although her mouth was trying to form the right words, the chemistry between them was still sizzling.

Even while struggling against a shockingly powerful urge to wring her neck, Angelos found himself being distracted by the smooth, creamy perfection of her skin and the way her full breasts pressed against her white shirt.

No wonder he hadn't been concentrating the night of the ball. *She was spectacular.*

Exasperated with himself, he forced his attention back to her eyes. 'Even if I wasn't already aware of your reputation, Isabelle, your performance at the ball would have been more than enough to convince me that, quite apart from being that "sort of woman", in fact your *specialist subject* is the inside of men's hotel rooms.'

'My reputation?' She sounded astonished, as though it were news to her that she *had* a reputation, and he gave her a warning glance.

'Now I know who you are, I can understand why you went to such extraordinary lengths not to introduce yourself. Next time you want to trap a billionaire, change your name.'

Her eyes widened, and suddenly he forgot everything that he'd been intending to say.

She had the most amazing eyes he'd ever seen. Standing this close, and with the benefit of the spring sunshine to light her face, he could see that the sapphire was broken by flecks of green— as if an adoring artist had been determined to do everything possible to increase the impact of those eyes on a woefully poorly prepared male race. And as for her body—

He gritted his teeth, aware that it had been her body that had contributed to the situation they now found themselves in. His libido had smothered the sound of alarm bells ringing in his head.

His comment silenced her for a moment and she watched him, her chest rising and falling under the white lace blouse.

Aware that the audience around them was listening intently to the entire conversation, Angelos reached out and slid an arm round her waist, jerking her against him.

'I'll give you some more free advice,' he murmured softly, his lips close to her ear. His actions were those of a lover, but his words were those of an aggressor, and he felt the sudden tension in her body, 'if you want a man to believe in your virtue, don't wear a skirt that reveals your chosen brand of underwear. Not that I'm complaining, you understand. If we have to do this, we might as well both enjoy it. In fact, I'm wondering what extras come with the waitress costume? Whipped cream? Melted chocolate?'

'Do what? What are you talking about?'

He felt her try to pull away and pressed his hand into the hollow of her back, distracted by how small her waist was. *How could anyone manage to be curvy and slender at the same time?*

'I'm talking about our new relationship, *agape mou.* The one you wanted so badly.'

'You're being ridiculous. Let me go.'

'Believe me, there's nothing I'd like more. But unfortunately I can't. Thanks to you, we're both in a situation that can't be easily solved. You're coming with me now, so that we can analyse our extremely limited options.' They were still locked together, the softness of her body pressed against the unyielding hardness of his, and he was finding it harder and harder to focus on what needed to be done. What had started as a means of ensuring that their conversation remained private had swiftly turned into something much, much more intimate.

It was like being back on the dance floor.

The scent of her skin and hair invaded his senses and he felt the immediate reaction of his body. Sexual awareness erupted and she obviously felt it too because she gave a moan of denial.

'Why would you want me to come with you? I seem to remember you telling me that you would rather be celibate than spend the rest of your life with a woman like me.'

He tensed. He'd flung those words at her on the night of the ball, and having them thrown back at him now was a harsh reminder of the realities of the current situation.

'I have no intention of spending the rest of my life with you. Just a few weeks. I'm sure that will be more than enough for both of us.'

'A few weeks?' She gave a brief shake of her head. 'I still have no idea what you're talking about, and my answer is still no.'

'So far I haven't asked you a question that needed an answer. Either you get in the car, or I'll lift you into it myself.'

'We have an audience who can see quite clearly that you are bullying me. Do you really think you can kidnap me in broad daylight?'

'No. I plan to be a great deal more subtle than that.' He brought his mouth down on hers and directed all the anger and frustration he was feeling into his kiss. But the moment her soft lips melded with his, his mind blanked and all control vanished. Her mouth was like a wicked, forbidden drug and even as he lost himself in the kiss he knew that the taste of her lips was going to stay with him for ever. Sweet, seductive, dangerously sinful—

Abruptly he lifted his head, astounded by his own ferocious hunger.

As he frowned down at her beautiful face, he noticed that her eyes were dazed and her cheeks were flushed. Her fingers were locked into the fabric of his shirt, as if for support.

Aware that he was fast approaching the point where he'd be prepared to risk a conviction for committing an indecent act in a public place, Angelos released her. 'No Parisian will intervene in a lovers' quarrel, *agape mou*. They know that the path of true love rarely runs smoothly, and by now they are all longing to see me ride roughshod over your objections and go for the happy ending.'

Without waiting for her response, he took her arm, controlling her easily with one hand while he used the other to open the car door.

As he propelled her into the passenger seat, a woman watching gave an envious sigh and turned to her friend.

'*L'amour*,' she said, and Angelos gave a grim smile as he slid into the driver's seat and started the engine.

Not *l'amour*, he thought viciously as he trod hard on the accelerator and made for the hotel.

Not *l'amour* at all.

What he had in mind had a much less romantic description attached to it.

CHAPTER THREE

WHAT did he want with her?

The living room of his penthouse suite was bigger than her entire flat, and looked out over the whole of Paris. It was a view that only the privileged few ever enjoyed, and at any other time Chantal would have been enchanted. But not now.

Her body was still in a state of helpless excitement following that one devastating kiss.

If dancing with him had been erotic, then kissing him had been—

She couldn't find a word for it.

Her legs still trembling, she looked around for somewhere solid to prop herself. She needed the support just in case he kissed her again.

But that wasn't going to happen, was it?

He wasn't even looking at her. Instead he was staring in brooding silence down into the streets below.

Her tongue sneaked out and touched her lower lip, still slightly swollen from the bruising force of his kiss. She was well aware that he'd used the kiss as a means of distracting their audience, but that knowledge in no way diminished the chemistry that had exploded between them.

Was the chemistry responsible for the anger she sensed in him?

The truth was, she no longer understood what was going on.

She'd attributed his anger on the night of the ball to the fact that he'd somehow discovered that she was an uninvited guest. When he'd first waved the crumpled ticket at her, she'd assumed that he was displaying the evidence.

And then he'd called her 'Isabelle', and she'd realised that he believed her to be the owner of the ticket. And the crazy thing was she didn't even *know* 'Isabelle'.

Obviously he didn't yet know that she'd gatecrashed the party.

Deeply regretting the impulse that had made her use a ticket that wasn't hers, Chantal glanced around furtively, half expecting someone in uniform to put a hand on her shoulder and arrest her.

Could you be arrested for something like that?

Did it count as identity theft if the transgression had only been for one short evening? Did it count as identity theft if the victim was none the wiser and the thief almost immediately gave the identity back? It wasn't really theft, was it? More a case of—borrowing. She'd borrowed someone else's name for a short time, just to see whether time and maturity had given her the confidence to mingle with people who'd used to make her feel insignificant.

Trying to ignore the shimmer of insecurity that had started to take hold, Chantal stood there awkwardly.

Now what?

Since he'd picked up her from the street, Angelos hadn't spoken a word. He'd strapped her with restrained violence into the passenger seat and proceeded to drive skilfully through the fast Paris traffic before finally pulling up outside the most expensive hotel in the city.

Only then had he finally glanced in her direction. His tone icy cold, he'd uttered just one word. 'Out.'

The simmer of anger in his dark eyes had made her insides quake, but remembering the few weeks she'd spent working in the hotel when she'd first arrived in Paris, she hadn't wanted to draw attention to herself by arguing with him on the pavement. So Chantal had simply lowered her head and followed him meekly into the lift that led directly to the penthouse suite, hoping that none of the staff would recognise her.

As soon as the door had closed behind them, she'd regretted following him and now she was finally alone with him she felt a flutter of nerves in her stomach.

She tried to look relaxed. *As if his kiss hadn't turned her insides into a mass of squirming, helpless longing.* 'All right. I'm here. What did you want to say to me?' *Why didn't he speak?* She just wished he'd say *something.* Anything—instead of just standing there with his back to her, his broad shoulders stiff with tension. 'Perhaps I should just leave—'

He turned, the angular lines of his handsome face set and hard. 'If you leave, I'll just bring you back.' He was autocratic and intimidating and she stood frozen to the spot, confused by the conflict she sensed in him.

He'd kissed her, but it was obvious that he wasn't happy about it.

'Let's just get one thing straight from the outset,' she muttered, deciding that she might as well make her position clear. 'I *won't* have sex with you, so if that's what this is all about, you might as well just let me go now.'

A protracted silence followed her impulsive declaration. The only indication that he'd even heard her was a slight narrowing of his dark eyes.

The silence unnerved her and she tried again. 'I'm just saying that although I'm sure every other woman you meet is desperate to—I mean, you're a good-looking guy, but...' Her voice trailed off, her chattiness extinguished by his total lack of response.

Finally, after what felt like a lifetime, he spoke.

'Do I look like the sort of man who picks up a woman from the street when he wants sex?'

Chantal could have told him that those men came in all shapes and sizes, but she chose to keep her thoughts to herself. 'I have no idea what sort of man you are. And I don't want to find out.'

'Really?' One dark eyebrow lifted in mockery. 'You expect me to believe that after the virtuoso performance you gave on the night of the ball?'

Remembering the erotic dance they'd shared, Chantal felt her heart-rate double. 'It was just a dance...' her voice trailed off again as his eyes locked on hers.

And suddenly there it was again.

The same silent connection that had drawn them together the night of the ball.

Something flickered in the depths of his eyes, something dark and dangerous, and she knew that his mind was in the same place as hers: *the exquisite agony of anticipation as their bodies had moved and slid together, the heat, the restrained passion, the delicious intimacy—*

They stared at each other until the tension in the room was wound so tightly that it came close to snapping.

This time he was the one to break the silence. 'Tell me something—' his voice was lethally soft '—is that how you trap all your men? You dance with them first? Is it your idea of a free trial? Try before you buy?'

His cynicism clashed with the image of him that her mind had greedily stored away. She'd remembered a gentleness, but there was nothing gentle about his man. He was all hard angles and sharp anger. 'I'm not for sale, Mr Zouvelekis.'

'I think the people who watched you dance might have trouble believing that.'

And the amazing thing was she hadn't been aware of anything or anyone but him. She'd been so absorbed by the rhythm of the music and the movement of his body that she'd been lost in her own world. The dance had been special. Something astonishing that they'd created together.

But that was ridiculous, of course. A prime example of her imagination running away yet again. For him, it hadn't been special. It had been a prelude to sex.

Not only was he turning the dance into something sleazy, he was judging her.

And although she didn't know anything about this Isabelle woman, she knew all about being judged.

Chantal straightened her shoulders. 'I danced because you insisted on it. *You* hauled me onto the dance floor like some possessive herd bull. But on that dance floor we were equally matched.' For a brief moment she'd experienced the bliss of having a man completely in tune with her. 'If I gave, then it's because you demanded. Whatever I did, you were there before me.'

'You manipulated the entire scenario. With a different man your plan might have worked.'

'I didn't have a plan. And *you* approached *me*.'

'You paraded yourself in front of me in a dress designed specifically to capture a man's attention.'

She decided that this wasn't the time to feel pride that her work on a length of material that had begun life dressing windows had been so successful and convincing. 'I didn't exactly *parade*.'

'Let me give you a few hints,' he purred, his lashes lowering to conceal the expression in his eyes. 'I'm Greek. I'm Greek all the way through. And when it comes to women we're still very traditional. Greek men like to do the choosing *and* the chasing.'

Chantal frowned, thinking about the article she'd read about him the day after the ball. 'I thought you were supposed to be very forward thinking. You have more women in executive positions than most companies.'

'That's business. In my personal life I'm very traditional,' he drawled. 'And it doesn't matter whether it's the boardroom or the bedroom, the important thing is to find the right woman for the

job. As far as wife material goes, you don't fit my ideal profile.
Next time spend more hours on your research.'

'Research?' Chantal shook her head in confusion. 'Did you
think you were some sort of *project*, or something?'

Contempt flickered across his features. 'Do you really think
that I haven't heard about you?'

So obviously Isabelle had a reputation as a gold-digger.

Floored by that piece of news, Chantal stood still, her brain
a hopeless tangle of indecision. It was obvious that she needed
to try once again to tell him that she wasn't this Isabelle person,
but doing that would mean admitting to an even worse crime. She
was a thief, and strictly speaking she'd impersonated someone
else. Could that be classed as fraud if the ticket had been in the
bin? Possibly. Could she go to gaol? Possibly. She didn't really
know, but she did know that he was angry enough to make
trouble.

Trouble that she didn't need.

Better a gold-digger than a thief.

Deciding that for the time being the less she revealed the
better, Chantal licked her lips. 'You're wrong about me.'

'Not wrong. It's obvious that you went to the ball with the intention of targeting me.'

Astonished by his interpretation of the facts, Chantal shook
her head. 'I didn't even know who you were until I picked up a
newspaper the next day.'

'Do you think I'm stupid?'

'Not stupid. Arrogant.'

'Realistic,' he shot back. 'And justifiably cautious. Clearly you
have no idea how many women have trodden that same path
before you. So I'll tell you once again that I could never be attracted to anyone as manipulative as you. Dishonesty is not a trait
I've ever admired in a woman.'

Chantal froze, doubly relieved that she hadn't told him the
truth.

He wouldn't understand, would he?

She cringed at the thought of the reaction that such a confession would invoke. This was a man with the world at his fingertips. What would someone like him know about her life? How could he even begin to understand what had driven her to do something like that?

A dark memory of the last time someone had discovered the truth about her rose, and she felt a flicker of the old panic. And then she reminded herself that her past was all safely hidden. It was buried so deep that no one would ever discover the truth about her. That part of her was gone for ever, and she was perfectly safe.

She was whoever she wanted to be.

And at the moment that might as well be Isabelle.

Trapped by a situation entirely of her own making, Chantal wiped her damp palms over the limited fabric of her skirt, wishing there was more of it. She felt horribly exposed—even more so as his gaze travelled slowly down the length of her legs.

She felt the same tingling feeling she'd felt the night of the ball and she lifted her chin, reminding herself that so far every second she'd spent with this man had been a disaster. '*Stop looking at me.*'

'If you don't want a man to look at you,' he bit out, 'try wearing a skirt that covers your bottom. If outfits could talk, then yours is saying "take me". You're a walking advert for sex. I'm surprised you haven't been arrested, walking the streets dressed in that. Or perhaps *un*dressed would be a better description.'

This was the point where she should tell him that she had until a few hours ago been working as a waitress. But she had no intention of doing that. And anyway, when had she ever allowed herself to be defined by her job? 'How I dress is my choice.'

'I agree absolutely,' he drawled, a cynical gleam in his dark eyes. 'But, having made that choice, you cannot then object when a man responds in a predictable way. We're not very

advanced when it comes to matters as basic as sex. You chose to
dress like that, and therefore it follows that you wanted to invoke
a certain reaction in the male sex. And that is entirely in keeping
with your reputation.'

Chantal felt a flicker of unease. What exactly had Isabelle
been up to?

It would have been helpful to know.

Apart from the obvious deduction that she was the sort of
woman willing to carelessly drop a coveted ticket in a hotel
dustbin, Chantal knew nothing about her. But her curious, inven-
tive mind had already started filling in the gaps. What had made
a woman discard a ticket to an event to which only a select few
were allowed access?

Who was she?

Judging from the derisive curl of Angelos's mouth, no one she
ever wanted to meet.

Chantal chewed her lip, trying not to reflect on the irony of
the fact that she'd obviously borrowed the identity of a woman
whose life was every bit as complex as her own.

Now what?

What should she do? Her whole life had been a web of lies
since childhood, but her lies were only self-protection, and they'd
never actually harmed anyone, had they? This was the first time
that any of her stories had caught up with her and she felt a flutter
of nerves in her stomach.

After their one explosive encounter she'd been left with the
impression that he wouldn't ever want to cross her path again.
Even now she didn't understand why he'd brought her here. At
first she'd assumed it was for sex, but there was nothing lover
like about the way he was glaring at her.

'So what do you want from me?' He came from a different
world, and that world still had the ability to shrink her back to a
terrified schoolgirl.

Victim.

The word flew into her head and she pushed it away immediately, straightening her shoulders.

She wasn't going to be anyone's victim. Never again.

Visibly tense, he tugged impatiently at the knot of his tie and undid the top button of his shirt, clearly finding it constricting. 'You are going to continue the charade that you began the night of the ball.'

'Sorry?'

Anger flashed in his dark eyes and his hand sliced through the air in a furious gesture. 'Do *not* pretend that you don't know what I'm talking about,' he breathed, 'when we *both* know that you used the ball as a means to meet me.'

'I've already told you that I didn't. I—'

'You virtually threw yourself across my path. And from the moment we met you couldn't stop looking at me.'

'Well, in order to have noticed you must have been looking at me too,' Chantal offered logically, and he inhaled sharply.

'You danced as though we were already horizontal in the bedroom.'

'You danced too.'

Her comment did nothing to alleviate his temper. He muttered something in Greek that she just *knew* would be better off not translated.

'I ought to congratulate you.' He switched back to English, his derisive tone suggesting that congratulations were the last thing on his mind. 'I thought I'd been on the receiving end of every possible trick, but you took the whole thing to an entirely new level.'

'You're obviously very angry, but—'

'You're right, I'm angry. Over the years various women have gone to enormous lengths to attract my attention. They pose as businesswomen, they apply for a job with me, they book tables in restaurants where I am dining, they hover outside my house in the hope of bumping into me. Sometimes they just turn up in my office wearing next to nothing, in the hope that they'll attract my attention.'

'Really?' Astonished that some women had the confidence to go to those lengths to meet someone, Chantal gaped at him. 'Gosh. That's amazing.'

'It is *not* amazing. It is intrusive and unacceptable.'

'It must be one of the drawbacks of being a billionaire, I suppose. Can't you laugh about it?'

He threw her an incredulous glance and sucked in a breath. 'It is not amusing. Particularly when a woman stoops so low as to target *my father* in order to gain my attention.'

'Ah.' Finally sensing the direction of the conversation, Chantal gave an awkward shrug. 'Actually, that wasn't exactly what happened.'

The expression on his handsome face was grim as he surveyed her. 'That is *exactly* what happened. Having danced with me, you then targeted him—like the greedy, unscrupulous, predatory woman you so clearly are.'

'I didn't know he was your father until you arrived with the drinks. And *he* approached *me*.'

'Of course he did. My father's fatal weakness is beautiful women—a fact of which you were well aware.'

'I knew nothing about your father until that night.' *Until he'd rescued her.* 'I really liked him.'

Angelos shot her a look so fierce it would have stopped a riot. 'I'm sure you did. He's rich. And you have a taste for rich men—don't you, Isabelle?'

'Do I?'

'Obviously. Given that you have already fleeced two in divorce settlements—one of them older than my father. For a woman of twenty six, you've been extremely busy.'

Chantal gasped. This Isabelle woman had married two men? One of them considerably older than her?

Perhaps continuing to let him believe that she was Isabelle hadn't been such a sensible idea, after all.

The situation was going from bad to worse, and it was obvious that she just needed to walk away from it and try and put the whole thing behind her.

'I'm obviously not your favourite person right now,' she ventured cautiously, 'so why am I here? Why did you come looking for me?'

'Because of the lies you told my father.'

'Lies?' Shrinking at the memory of that particular conversation, Chantal stood there helplessly. She couldn't explain without revealing things about herself that she'd spent her life concealing.

'You told him that we were in love—that you fell in love with me the first moment you saw me. Is it coming back to you yet, or do you need me to carry on?'

'Well—I didn't exactly—it was more that he assumed—'

A muscle flickered in his lean jaw. 'And did you correct him?'

Chantal breathed in and out. 'No.'

'Of course you didn't.' His tone was silky smooth. 'Presumably because your plan was all coming together nicely.'

'How does talking to your father bring me closer to marrying you?' Chantal wondered briefly what had made him so suspicious of women.

'You saw his face. You saw how delighted he was when he thought we were together.'

'He's obviously very keen to see you married,' Chantal said, her expression softening at the thought of his father. 'But I'm sure when you explained that it was all a misunderstanding he understood.'

Angelos tensed and turned away from her, his broad shoulders rigid with tension. 'Unfortunately I wasn't able to do that.'

'Why not?'

He turned back to face her and a muscle flickered in his lean jaw. 'My father had a heart attack that night. He was in hospital here in Paris for a week and then I had him flown back to Greece.'

'No!' Genuinely distressed by that piece of news, Chantal lifted her hand to her mouth and shook her head. 'Please tell me that isn't true—'

His eyes darkened ominously. 'You think I would joke about such a thing?'

'No! I just—' She felt as though something was crumbling inside her and she rubbed her fingers across her forehead, trying desperately to pull herself together. What was the matter with her? He wasn't *her* father. It was ridiculous to feel this way. 'I'm sorry. It's just that—is he going to be all right?'

'Why would you care?'

'Because I liked him so much. Is he recovering?'

'According to the doctors, his recovery so far has been nothing short of miraculous. Apparently he has been clinging to life, determined to live long enough to witness my marriage to the wonderful woman he saw me with that night at the ball.' His tone was acid. 'It seems that our "relationship" has given him a reason to live.'

'I'm glad he's going to be all right, but—' Chantal stared at him in growing dismay as his words sunk in '—you didn't—you haven't told him the truth, then?'

'What do you think?'

That he was a man who loved his father. Greek. Family mattered to Greeks. 'Obviously you didn't want to as he was poorly, and no one would blame you for that.' Feeling awkward, she cleared her throat. 'So that means he still thinks that we—that we're—'

'In love,' Angelos slotted in helpfully. 'Crazy about each other. All the things you told him that night. When he finally regained consciousness he distracted himself from the stresses of hospital by lying in bed naming his grandchildren.'

'Oh—' Chantal breathed out heavily and thought quickly.

'So obviously you're waiting to find the right time to explain that there was a misunderstanding?'

'And when do you think he'd like to hear that piece of unwelcome news?' His tone was biting. 'Before or after his next heart attack—which, according to the specialists, is a distinct possibility.'

Chantal was horrified. 'I seriously hope they're wrong about that.'

'So,' he said grimly, 'do I.'

'I hope he's resting.'

'He is currently staying on my island in Greece.'

'Your island?' *He had an island?* It was just as well she hadn't known who he was, Chantal thought weakly, because she never would have had the courage to talk to him in the first place. 'He's on his own on an island? Is that the best place for him?'

'He has a team of nurses and doctors attending to him and I intend to join him shortly.'

'Well, in that case—' she licked her lips '—I'm sure once you're there you'll find the right time to tell him that we're not exactly—together.'

'I don't intend to tell him. Not until he's well. On the contrary, the doctors have instructed that he should be kept as relaxed as possible over the coming weeks. No stresses. No worries. He should be surrounded by people he loves and trusts.'

'Right. Well, that sounds sensible.' Chantal stared at him. 'So— what does this have to do with me?'

His mouth tightened. 'Unfortunately for both of us you played your game rather well the night of the ball. My father enjoyed your company enormously. He is looking forward to your arrival on the island so that he can get to know his future daughter-in-law.'

CHAPTER FOUR

SHE LOOKED the picture of innocence, Angelos thought savagely. There was a gentleness in her eyes and a softness to her face that was totally at odds with her reputation as a man-eater. Not just a man-eater, he reminded himself grimly. Her tastes were more refined than that. She was a clever, manipulative, rich-man-eater.

'He thinks we're getting married?' Her eyes were wide and shocked, and Angelos fought back his distaste.

He couldn't believe he'd actually allowed himself to be manipulated in this way. Only once in his life before had he ever been taken in by a woman, and on that occasion he'd had inexperience as his excuse. He'd been just eighteen years of age, and dizzy with lust. Lust—love—how easily those two became intertwined. His mouth tightened at the thought.

He was no longer eighteen.

So what was his excuse this time?

He resisted the temptation to turn the full force of his anger onto the woman standing in front of him. 'You told him that you were crazy about me. That we were madly in love.' Angelos struggled to keep his voice level. 'As far as my father is concerned, the next step is marriage.'

Her gaze softened. 'He is *such* a lovely man. I thought that at the time.'

I'll just bet you did. Angelos made a mental note not to leave her alone with his father for too long. Despite her protests, he had no doubt that once she discovered her 'relationship' with him had no long-term prospects she would have no compunction about turning her attentions to his more vulnerable father. 'Before you start congratulating yourself on your success, remember that this is *me* you're dealing with—not my father.'

'You want me to go to Greece with you? That's what you've brought me here to ask me?'

'I don't *want* you to go to Greece with me. But that is what is going to happen.'

Obviously the two men she'd duped hadn't been able to see past those sapphire eyes, he thought grimly. And this time she'd obviously decided to go for the jackpot. The sheer audacity of her plan amazed even him. His views on marriage were well known, as were his views on his father's two very public and very expensive divorces. The fact that she'd believed that she might be successful said a great deal about her ego.

'I don't understand why you would think it's a good idea. Your father would never believe that we were together!'

'Thanks to your convincing display at the ball, he *already* believes that we are together,' Angelos told her. 'Your role is simply to produce more of the same. It shouldn't be too hard. I'll be working for most of the day. You will get to sit by a pool with a drink in your hand and a view of the Aegean Sea, singing my praises. From what I can gather, you're in between men at the moment. Think of it as a free holiday—which isn't quite on the same level as a meal ticket for life, but given the stunt you pulled you're lucky even to get that from me.'

She watched him, and he could almost see her brain working as she thought about what he'd said.

'No.'

'Don't try and negotiate with me,' he warned softly. 'There won't be a better offer.'

'I'm not hoping for a "better offer".'

'Then why refuse?'

'Because it wouldn't be fair on your father. I don't understand why you think it's a good idea.' She frowned slightly. 'When he finds out that you're lying, he'll be devastated.'

The same uncomfortable truth had occurred to Angelos, but he'd been unable to find any other solution. 'It is a shame this conscience of yours didn't emerge a little sooner. Thanks to you, I don't have a choice. When my father is stronger, I'll tell him that we weren't as compatible as we thought.'

'It would never work.'

'Why not?'

'If you glare at me the way you're glaring at me now, he's never going to be convinced that our relationship is real.'

'The mere fact that I am bringing you to the island will be enough to convince him.'

'Why?'

Angelos tensed. 'I don't take women there.'

Her eyebrows rose. 'Never?'

'It is a place for family.'

'And none of your previous women have earned that distinction?'

'You are not family either, Isabelle,' Angelos warned her softly. 'Do not forget that. You're merely a necessary part of my father's convalescence.'

She frowned. 'I'm not sure—'

'I don't understand why you're hesitating. I'm offering you an all-expenses-paid luxury holiday.'

She looked at him, her gaze disturbingly direct. 'That's why I'm hesitating.'

He thought he could buy her.

But she didn't accept gifts from men, or hospitality. Ever. She lived her life by that principle.

Chantal gave a shiver, acknowledging the irony of her situation. She'd taken the ticket of a woman who clearly didn't share her scruples.

'I can't do it,' she said hoarsely and his eyes narrowed.

'You *will* do it—if I have to drag you there myself.'

'No. My answer has to be no.' Something dark and ugly uncurled inside her and she gave a little shake of her head. 'You don't understand.'

'I understand perfectly. And that's what frightens you, isn't it? For once you're dealing with a man who *does* understand you. All your declarations about liking my father have proved to be as meaningless and empty as I believed them to be.'

'That isn't true.'

'If it were true then you would be doing everything possible to aid his recovery.'

Chantal turned away, remembering just how kind his father had been to her that night of the ball. She remembered the warmth of his hand on hers and how he'd stood next to her, protecting her.

She owed him her help. She *wanted* to help. But how could she when helping meant accepting Angelos's hospitality?

The obvious solution would be to pay for herself, but given the pathetic state of her finances that wouldn't be possible. She might be able to scrape together enough to cover the cost of her flight ticket, but there was no way she'd have anything left over to cover her living costs.

'The fact that you are even hesitating shows me that you are every bit as cold-hearted as your reputation suggests.' His tone was harsh. 'I have explained that your presence would help my father, but as usual all you are thinking of is yourself.'

Stung by the injustice of that accusation, Chantal turned. 'That is not true.' She lifted her fingers to her forehead, trying to think the situation through.

Would it be so very wrong to say yes?

It wasn't as if she and Angelos were having an affair. Despite

the chemistry between them, it wasn't that sort of relationship.
All they'd ever shared was one dance and a lot of cross words.
She would be living in the villa as a favour to him. To help his
father.

That was quite different from—

Pushing aside her reservations, she gave a swift nod. 'I'll do
it. But I insist on paying for my flight ticket.'

A stunned expression crossed his handsome face and then he
gave a humourless laugh. 'It's a little late to try and impress me,'
he drawled, 'and anyway, I don't issue tickets when I fly by
private jet.'

The colour poured into her cheeks and she felt a rush of humiliation. Private jet. Of course. How could she have been so
stupid? She should have known that this man wouldn't exactly
fly budget airlines.

'Wait—what I mean is, I don't want you paying for me,' she
stammered, and he raised an eyebrow.

'I could probably calculate your share if you wanted me to.
But it would have several noughts attached to it. If you're trying
to persuade me that you're not interested in my wealth, then
you're wasting your time. The evidence is stacked against you.'

Chantal bit her lip. She didn't have the money to reimburse
him for the flight, so she couldn't push the point, but she felt
deeply uncomfortable.

'If I come with you—' she lifted her chin and looked him in
the eye '—it's just because of your father. Not for any other
reason.'

'What other reason would there be? I'm not like the other men
you've met, Isabelle. It takes more than a little hot chemistry to
cloud my judgement.'

Uncomfortably aware of his scrutiny, she blushed and walked
across to the window, turning her back to him.

He was so different from his father. Hard where his father had
been soft. Intimidating where his father had been approachable.

Remembering just how much she'd liked the older man, she felt something tug deep inside her and felt a sudden pang of regret that he was now so poorly.

She remembered how delighted he'd seemed that his son was 'in love' and her expression softened. Clearly the son hadn't inherited his knife-sharp cynicism from his father.

From her vantage point on the balcony, Chantal stared down at the streets of Paris. She could see the Seine, winding through the city, and the bold jut of the Eiffel Tower, its structure glinting in the warm sunshine.

And across the city, in the dirtiest, cheapest, most forgotten part of Paris, was the room that she'd vacated that morning. The price had become prohibitive. Too much for a waitress. It was time to move on.

Why not to Greece? She had no other place to go. Nowhere else she needed to be.

Wouldn't that solve all her problems in the short term as well as helping out a man she genuinely cared about?

If her presence helped his recovery, then wasn't that reason enough to go?

She could stay as long as she was needed, and then use Greece as a base for her next adventure. The only drawback was being in the company of Angelos Zouvelekis. He unsettled her more than any man she'd ever met.

But he'd be working, wouldn't he? *Adding more noughts to his billions?*

All she had to do during the day was lie by the pool and chat to his father.

'You'll have to tell him the truth at some point.'

'Obviously. But not until he is stronger and has something else to focus on. Having had such a close brush with death, it seems that the only thing on his mind is the fact that I haven't yet given him grandchildren. When he is properly recovered he will find something else to occupy him.'

She turned. 'You don't intend to give him grandchildren?'

'At some point. But only when I find a woman whose genes I would be proud for my children to inherit.' His tone left her in no doubt that he wouldn't be allowing *her* genes anywhere near his offspring.

And that was an attitude she was more than familiar with.

She'd never fitted in, had she?

All her life she'd felt displaced.

As a child she'd lived her life around the edges of a world to which she didn't belong. And rarely had anyone shown her kindness.

His father had shown her kindness.

'I'll do it,' she said firmly. 'If you think it will help.'

'It never occurred to me that you wouldn't,' he drawled, contempt flickering in his eyes. 'From what I've heard, you never spend your money if you can spend someone else's.'

She tensed. 'I'm doing this for your father.'

'Of course you are. Your generosity is legendary.'

Chantal was almost relieved that she wasn't Isabelle. 'No matter what you think,' she said quietly, 'I'm not interested in your money.'

It had been something else entirely that had drawn her to him. A powerful connection that she couldn't explain. A chemistry that taunted both of them, because it was something that neither wanted to pursue.

The Aegean Sea stretched beneath them, the changing light producing more shades of blue than an artist's palette.

'It's beautiful,' she murmured, but she was talking to herself—because Angelos had been on the phone since his private jet had lifted off from Paris. And he was still on the phone. He lounged on a sofa opposite her, his eyes fixed on a computer screen, the table in front of him strewn with papers. Occasionally he broke the conversation for long enough to scan a set of figures, then he was talking again, in rapid Greek.

He'd paid her no attention whatsoever.

And perhaps that was just as well, she reflected, because her astonishment and awe when she'd seen the inside of his private jet had bordered on the gauche.

She had no idea how Isabelle would have reacted, but her mouth had dropped open in disbelief as she'd taken in the sumptuous cream leather sofas and the soft carpeting.

If it hadn't been for the uniformed cabin attendant's instruction to fasten her seat belt, she would have believed that it was all a mistake and she was actually in a high-class apartment. She'd been afraid to eat or drink in case she dropped something and her one trip to the bathroom had left her wishing she'd had time to design herself a new wardrobe.

By contrast, Angelos had merely divested himself of the jacket of his suit, loosened his tie, and ordered a black coffee.

Greek coffee, she assumed, staring at the thick black grounds that remained in the bottom of his cup.

Her most anxious moment had occurred when he'd asked for her passport. But she needn't have worried because he'd simply handed it straight to one of his staff—a woman who clearly had no idea which name was supposed to be inside the document.

Since then he hadn't looked at her. Hadn't once asked after her comfort. Hadn't even hurled an insult in her direction or given her one of his looks.

It was almost as if he preferred to think she didn't exist.

Which had made her journey more comfortable, but didn't bode well for the roles they were supposed to play.

His last few moments of freedom, she mused, wondering how he was ever going to manage to maintain this charade once they arrived at his island.

She waited until he'd terminated his latest phone call and then spoke. 'Are we pretending to be lovers who have had a row?'

He glanced up from the figures he was scanning, his thick dark lashes drawing attention to his eyes. 'A row?'

'We are supposed to be adding to your father's relaxation. I don't think being with two people who react to each other in stony silence is going to do much for his peace of mind. If we *were* already married, then I think divorce would be looming.'

His eyes narrowed, and he dropped the paper onto the table. 'When I need to talk to you, I'll talk.'

'Fine. But there are a few things I need to know if I'm going to stand any chance of being convincing.'

'Such as?'

'Details. Facts. The sort of things that would have come up in conversation. Does anyone else live on the island, or is it just you?'

He leaned back in his chair. 'Stop pretending you're not already in possession of a full list of my assets.'

Chantal sighed. Clearly a woman like Isabelle would have known the answer to that question. 'Has it ever occurred to you that you might have misjudged me?'

'No. Why would it?' He tucked his pen back into his pocket. 'Don't even *think* about playing any of your usual games.'

'Don't worry.' Having no idea what Isabelle's usual games were, Chantal kept her answer suitably vague. 'I'm just going to lie by the pool and chat to your father.'

'And don't get any ideas on that score, either.'

'What?' She felt a flicker of exasperation. 'I thought that was what you wanted me to do?'

'Your role is to convince my father that we are a happy couple. I'm well aware that your taste can run to older men if the price is right. In this case, don't even think about it.'

It took her a moment to grasp his meaning. 'Are you suggesting that I'm interested in your *father*?'

'You seemed interested enough the night of the ball. You were all over him. Flirting.'

'*Talking.*'

'Laughing. Asking him to dance.'

'I liked him. He was kind to me.' *And so few people in her life had ever been kind to her.*

'My father is kind to everyone.'

'And you disapprove of that quality?'

'When it comes to glamorous women it's a weakness, not a quality.'

'If everyone was kinder to each other the world would be a better place.'

He gave a cynical laugh. 'And we both know what form you'd want that kindness to take. As you already know, my father is a rich man. Not quite as rich as I am, but I've no doubt you were happy to consider him good enough for back-up.'

Appalled and fascinated by the thought of what might drive a woman to such desperation, Chantal studied him for a moment. Her response was cautious. 'That's what you think I'd do?'

'Given that your last husband was seventy-five—yes.'

Seventy five? Chantal almost gasped aloud. Isabelle had married a man of *seventy-five*? She wondered briefly whether she should have told the truth about who she was. No. If he was shocked by Isabelle, how much more shocked would he be to learn the truth about *her* life?

'I'm just warning you not to try any tricks, because I'll be watching.'

'Tricks? What tricks are you expecting?'

'You've failed with me. Don't even think about targeting my father. A man who has made two mistakes in marriage will not be allowed to make a third!'

'Mistake?' She blinked at him. 'He told me that he was married to your mother for forty years. It didn't sound like a mistake to me. He was totally in love.' She watched as shock flared in his eyes.

'You asked him about my *mother*?'

'No! He—' Thrown by his anger, she broke off, struggling to remember exactly how the conversation had evolved. 'We were talking about love. He told me that she died. I—I'm very sorry.'

He didn't respond, but she saw that his knuckles were white. 'He *never* talks about my mother.'

'Well, he talked to *me*. Maybe it was because I was a stranger. Or because we just seemed to click. I don't know. I *liked* him—' She gave a helpless shrug. 'Why do you dissect every conversation? Who made you so cynical?'

'Women like you. I know who you are, Isabelle.'

He had no idea who she was.

And she had no intention of telling him. Perhaps one day he'd find out, when he bumped into the real Isabelle on the party circuit. But by then she'd be long gone.

She sank back against her seat. He intimidated her, but at the same time he intrigued her, and suddenly she really wanted to understand what drove his deep-rooted cynicism. Something in his past, obviously. She, better than anyone, knew that even when you tried to move on the past had a way of winding itself around your ankles like seaweed—taking hold, *dragging you back to the place you were trying to escape from.*

'So—' she changed the subject to a topic less inflammatory '—what do you do with a whole island to yourself?'

'It has been in my family for five generations. My ancestors grew olives and made wine. I rebuilt the villa five years ago. It is the one place where we can guarantee a level of privacy, away from media intrusion.'

'Five generations?' Chantal felt a flash of envy. What must it be like to have family you could trace back for generations? What was it like to be part of a group of people who cared about each other?

'They led a simple life,' he told her, stretching his legs out in front of him, 'and that is what the island is for. So if you're hoping for a glamorous holiday, then you'll be disappointed. The only thing that glitters is the sea when the sun hits it. You can leave your silk and diamonds at home. We don't dress for dinner. It's basic. I prefer it that way.'

So did she.

Chantal relaxed slightly. The dress code had been one of her major concerns about this trip. Given the deficiencies of her wardrobe, the thought of 'dressing for dinner' had filled her with dismay. And as for leaving her silk or diamonds at home—not only did she not possess any silk and diamonds, she didn't have a permanent home in which to leave them.

'It sounds perfect.'

'Don't be ridiculous. We both know you're going to hate it. I think we're about to discover just how "adaptable" you are, Isabelle.'

Probably a great deal more adaptable than he thought.

She braced herself as the plane came into land. 'Is this it?'

'No.' He unfastened his seat belt and rose to his feet. 'There is no landing strip on the island; it's too mountainous and craggy. We take a boat from here. So if you've any thoughts of running away, you're going to be disappointed. Unless you develop fins and a tail, once you're on the island you're stuck there.'

Angelos felt the spray on his face and increased the power, revelling in the sudden surge that had the luxury speedboat bouncing over the water, leaving a line of foam in its wake.

This stretch of sea was notoriously rough, but he didn't slacken the pace. Instead he steered the boat bows-on to the dancing waves.

Would the woman be seasick?

For a moment he almost relished what lay ahead.

Someone like her, who preyed on vulnerable men, would be frustrated and out of her depth on the island. There would be no one to seduce.

And not only that she'd been forced to leave all her seduction tools behind, he thought, smiling to himself as he contemplated what the mixture of seaspray and wind must be doing to her hair.

With a certain sadistic pleasure, he glanced over his shoulder—and felt a flash of surprise. Her hair was blowing wildly in the wind, but instead of clutching at it, as he'd expected, she was resting her head back against the safety rail of the boat and her eyes were closed.

She looked strangely content. Which made no sense at all.

He glanced towards the one small bag she'd brought aboard the flight from Paris. Her lack of luggage was a clear indication that she expected to be taken on some serious shopping trips— which meant that she was going to be severely disappointed. They weren't going anywhere, and she would be forced to wear whatever items she'd brought with her. And wear them again. And again. And launder them herself.

Angelos smiled as he thought about the role that she was going to be expected to play as his prospective wife.

Knowing his father, the first thing he'd want to see would be her prowess in the kitchen.

Can she cook, Angelos?

Undoubtedly not. In fact, he was willing to bet she'd never been near a hot stove in her life, let alone slaved over one. Why would she, when the men she'd married had given her a lifestyle beyond her wildest dreams?

If she'd had any sense she would have taken the money from her last divorce and settled in the Caribbean, instead of moving on to her next victim.

As they drew closer to the island Angelos slowed the boat and pulled in alongside the jetty. He cut the engine, and the air was filled with the insistent rasp of cicadas.

Above them he glimpsed the whitewashed walls of the villa. Hot pink bougainvillaea tumbled joyfully over the walls, basking in the hot Greek sunshine, and the path that led up from the jetty was thickly bordered with blue agapanthus.

'Home.'

It was only when she looked at him that he realised he'd spoken the word aloud.

'Is it home? I thought you lived in Athens?'

'My business requires that I travel a lot and I have a home in Athens because my headquarters is based there. But I have offices in almost all the major cities in the world. It's a necessity.'

'You don't like the city?'

'Sometimes. But the villa feels more like home than any other property I own. It is the place we spend time as a family.' He didn't know which surprised him more. His own confession or her nod of immediate understanding.

'I can see why you love it. It's beautiful.'

It seemed such an unlikely response from a woman with a love of the bright lights that he felt a flicker of irritation and suddenly regretted that circumstances had forced him to bring her with him. The island was usually a place to escape from the stresses and demands of his life. This time he'd been forced to bring the stress along with him.

He was about to make a sharp comment when he caught sight of the expression on her face. Her eyes sparkled with excitement and she was staring at the white-pebbled beach as though she couldn't wait to slip her shoes off and take a walk.

Surprised by her reaction, Angelos frowned. Pretty though it was, the island was a long way from the mainland. There were no trendy cafes, no boutique hotels or designer shops. No men and no nightclubs. In fact, nothing to entertain a woman like Isabelle. Just beaches, olives groves and dusty tracks winding their way over the headland.

He'd expected to see boredom or impatience on her face. Certainly not excitement. Suddenly she seemed vivid and alive and his eyes were drawn to the thrust of her breasts under the thin white top. Her body was lush and feminine, her mouth full and tempting, and her eyes were shining with almost child-like enthusiasm.

Angelos tightened his jaw, not knowing whether to be amused or irritated by the powerful and predictable response of his body.

Was he really that shallow?

Obviously the answer to that question was yes.

With a cynical laugh at his own expense, he turned away and secured the boat to the jetty with the rope.

It was ironic, he reflected, that the woman he'd finally brought home to this island was probably the last person on earth he'd contemplate marrying.

But, just as long as he kept that fact from his father, there shouldn't be a problem.

Feeling the heat of the sun on the back of her neck, Chantal followed Angelos up the path that led from the jetty to the villa. The garden seemed to tumble down the hillside, a joyful haven so breathtakingly beautiful that she paused for a moment just to enjoy the scent and colour. Orange and magnolia trees bordered the path, and the sea sparkled turquoise in the dazzling sunlight.

Aware that Angelos was glaring at her impatiently, she hurried towards him, followed him round a bend in the path and had her first proper view of the villa.

It had obviously been built to give the owners the benefit of what must surely be the best views in Greece, and her first impression left her speechless with wonder.

Between the villa and the sea lay a series of terraces, shaded by vines and linked by narrow paths. And on the same level as the villa itself was a large curved pool which followed the shape of the hillside and which appeared to merge with the ocean beyond.

Despite its obvious size, the villa itself was a vision of Mediterranean charm. Bougainvillaea tumbled from balconies, down over whitewashed walls to the scented gardens below. On the ground floor an arched entrance offered a tantalising view of a shaded stone courtyard with a central fountain. Doors opened from the main living area to the pool and inside the spacious room she could see rich-coloured textiles set against cool white walls.

'Kalispera!' A nurse appeared, wearing a crisp white uniform and a stern expression on her face.

Angelos walked towards her. 'How is my father today?'

'Determined to do himself as much damage as possible!' The nurse set her mouth in a disapproving line, and Angelos lifted an eyebrow.

'His tests are not good?'

'His tests are excellent, but he refuses to make any changes to his lifestyle.' Clearly exasperated with her patient, the nurse glanced at Chantal. 'Perhaps you will be able to influence him. He's been very excited about your arrival. Hopefully now you are here he will join you for dinner. I couldn't persuade him to eat lunch.'

Angelos frowned. 'He isn't eating?'

'He doesn't have much of an appetite.' Her tone sharp, the nurse flipped through her notebook, checking her facts. 'Black coffee for breakfast, nothing for lunch, and now he's asking for a drink.'

'Presumably not water?' Angelos said wearily. 'All right. I'll talk to him.'

'I'd appreciate that.' The nurse gave a brief nod and slipped the book back into her pocket. 'I'll go and talk to the kitchen about his diet. See if there's anything we can make that might tempt him.'

Angelos took Chantal's arm and steered her towards the pool. It was set high enough up to give a breathtaking view of the bay and several small islands in the distance, and for a moment she just stood there, wondering if there was a place more peaceful or beautiful anywhere on earth. She'd travelled, and seen many sights, but there was something about this place that made her catch her breath.

'It's stunning.'

Angelos turned towards her and smiled and that smile was so intimate and sexy that her stomach flipped. For a moment she was blinded. The world around her shrank and there was nothing but him. No view, no villa, no other person. She just gazed back at him, the words in her mouth melting away unspoken.

She was just reminding herself of the need to breathe when he leaned towards her, a smile in his eyes as his lips brushed against her cheek.

'Don't get too comfortable. I'm watching you,' he murmured softly in her ear, and she realised then that the smile and the sudden softening in his eyes had been for the benefit of his father, who was beaming with delight as he watched them.

And she took a step backwards, confused and disorientated because for one deeply humiliating moment she'd actually believed that the smile was for her.

And then she remembered. *Men like him didn't smile at women like her*.

Reminding herself of the dangers of slipping into fantasy land, she stepped away from him and walked to his father, automatically gravitating towards a friendly face. 'It's good to see you again, Mr Zouvelekis.'

'Call me Costas. After all, we're virtually family.' The older man struggled to his feet. Then he took her hands and squeezed, and the pressure of his fingers and the warmth in his eyes made the breath catch in her throat.

To be shown affection was such a rare and surprising gift that she clung to his fingers, unwilling to end a contact that felt so good.

Virtually family.

Never in her most extravagant fantasies would she have allowed herself to imagine a father as amazing as him. 'How are you?' Looking at him now, she could see that he'd lost weight and that his face had a greyish tinge.

'Better now I have something beautiful to look at. The nurses Angelos found—' He peered around him to check that the nurse was out of earshot and then pulled a face. 'He might as well have employed men.'

'Believe me, I tried,' Angelos said sternly. 'You're not supposed to be looking at the nurses.'

'I'm not.' Costas sounded gloomy. 'What is there to look at? That woman has the appeal of a wrestler. If she gets bored with nursing she could be a prison governor. Why did you employ her?'

'I employed her because her credentials are excellent. She tells me you haven't been eating.'

'She is a spy,' Costas grumbled, still holding Chantal's hands. 'Yesterday I tipped my medicine into a plant, and she immediately delivered another dose. *Obviously* she was watching from the bushes.'

Chantal chuckled. 'So that's why the garden is looking so good.'

Costas laughed too. Only Angleos wasn't amused.

'I'm paying her to make sure you make a full recovery.'

'If life is going to be this tedious I'm not sure that I want to. Still—' Costas lifted both Chantal's hands to his lips and kissed them gallantly. 'You're here now, and that changes everything.'

'Take your hands *off* my woman,' Angelos drawled, his expression faintly exasperated as he firmly removed Chantal's hands from his father's and enclosed them in a cool, hard grip. 'It isn't good for your blood pressure.'

'You have nothing to fear from me, Angelos.' His father looked suddenly tired, but the smile lingered in his eyes. 'The way she was looking at you a moment ago—no one else existed. That is how love should be. A woman in love can be in a crowd of handsome men, but she sees only one of them.'

Realising that it was true, Chantal felt suddenly vulnerable. She'd looked at Angelos. And he'd looked at her. The difference was that Angelos had been acting a part, whereas her reaction had been genuine. For a moment she'd forgotten that none of this was real. Staring into his eyes, she'd been taken straight back to those endless minutes on the dance floor, where their connection had been disturbingly intense and entirely genuine. The attraction between them had been primal and instinctive, undiluted by the complications of identity.

Costas sank into the nearest chair, as if standing was just too much. 'We haven't even been officially introduced.'

'I'm Chantal,' she said, and then caught the sardonic lift of Angelos's brows and knew instantly what he was thinking. *That she was embarrassed to admit her true identity.*

And the irony of the situation wasn't lost on her. She'd spent her life trying to be someone different, but now that she'd been offered a genuine alias she didn't want to take it.

She didn't want to be a woman who took money from a man.

It wasn't that she aspired to be perfect. Far from it. But that was the one sin she wasn't prepared to commit.

Maybe if Isabelle had been someone different she would have sat comfortably in her shoes for a few days, but as it was she was beginning to wonder whether her failure to confess her identity had been a mistake.

Costas sat for a moment, his weathered hand clutching the edge of the table.

Angelos stepped closer, a frown in his eyes. 'Are you unwell?' There was no missing the sharp anxiety in his voice, and Chantal found herself experiencing the same anxiety.

Costas Zouvelekis looked drained and exhausted, as if almost all of the life had been drained from him. She remembered him as an energetic, good-humoured man, and was shocked that his illness could have wrought such changes in such a short time.

'I'm fine. Don't fuss.' He glared at Angelos, and there was

pride in his eyes. Then he said something in Greek, and Chantal knew from the sudden tension in Angelos's powerful frame that Costas had been talking about her.

'I'm sure you have family matters you want to discuss, so I'll just—'

'You are family.' Costas gestured to the chair opposite. 'Sit down, and Maria will fetch you a drink to celebrate the occasion. The day my son finally brings a girl to his real home. Until I saw you in the boat I still couldn't believe it would happen. You have made me a very, *very* happy man.'

The nurse stepped out onto the terrace. 'You should take a nap before dinner, Mr Zouvelekis.'

Costas scowled. 'Nap? What am I? A baby?' But he rose to his feet swiftly, as if relieved that someone had suggested it. His gaze softened as he looked at Chantal. 'I would feel guilty leaving you when you've only just arrived, but I'm sure Angelos will find a way of entertaining you in the meantime.' His saucy wink implied that he knew exactly what form that entertainment was likely to take, but Angelos simply smiled as he strolled forward and helped his father to his feet.

Chantal watched the two of them, envy closing her throat. So it hadn't been her imagination. Angelos *was* capable of gentleness. It was there in his eyes when he talked to his father, and it stayed there until his father was safely in the villa and out of sight.

Only then did he turn to her, and the sudden chill in his eyes was a blunt reminder that she was only here because of his love for her father.

'Chantal?' His voice heavy with emphasis, Angelos sat back in his chair and contemplated her with ill-concealed mockery in his eyes. 'Changing the name doesn't change the person, *agape mou*. Remember that.'

'Chantal is my name.'

He smiled and reached for the jug of iced fruit juice that

Maria had placed on the table in front of them. 'I should imagine that it's useful to have more than one name.'

His contempt for her stung, and she rose to her feet. 'I think I'll go and shower and change.'

'Sit down.' His voice was so soft that it barely reached her ears, but there was no missing the authority in his tone and she sat in automatic response.

Only afterwards did she wonder why she'd responded without question.

'Do you expect everyone to obey you?'

'No. In fact I enjoy being challenged. There is no point in winning if there is no one else in the race.'

It was the sort of remark she'd come to expect of him. He was so confident about everything. *So sure of himself.* There was no doubt in her mind that this man had never felt out of place in his life. 'If you're bored, then please feel free to go and find something more interesting to do,' she muttered. 'Don't feel you have to entertain me. I'll be perfectly fine on my own.'

In fact she wished he *would* leave her on her own, because then she could talk some sense into herself. She found him incredibly, impossibly distracting and it was ridiculous to feel this way when he clearly considered the chemistry between them to be nothing short of an inconvenience.

Looking at his dark, luxuriant lashes and his wide, sensuous mouth, she felt the strength ooze from her body. *She just wanted him to kiss her.*

Those dark eyes locked on hers and the strength of the connection between them was so powerful that it shook her. 'My father likes you.'

'And I like him.' Her mouth was dry and her heart was thumping. 'He's an extremely nice man.'

They were talking about his father, but she knew, *she just knew*, that he was as distracted as she was. The chemistry between them was a living thing, a wild and dangerous force, curling itself around them like a million invisible threads.

Did he want to kiss her, too?

Was he thinking what she was thinking?

As if in answer to her question, Angelos dropped his gaze to her mouth and his eyes darkened. '"Nice" is a non-descriptive word that should almost always be substituted with something more specific. What are you trying to say? That's he's rich? Quite handsome for his age?'

They were talking, and yet an entirely different conversation was going on between them—one that didn't involve words. The air vibrated with the force of it, and Chantal's nerves were strained tight. She didn't understand what was happening. It wasn't as if they were flirting. In fact, the words they were exchanging were barely civil.

'I'm trying to say that he's kind and approachable.' The heat around them rose to stifling proportions and her heart thumped uncomfortably. The atmosphere made her feel so jumpy that she was about to stand up in an attempt to disturb the tension when Maria walked onto the terrace and quietly informed Angelos that he was needed on the phone.

Her words shattered the explosive atmosphere and achieved what neither of them had managed to achieve by themselves.

With a sharply indrawn breath, Angelos rose to his feet. 'It will be the Athens office.' He looked at Chantal, but his glance was brief, as if he didn't trust himself to look for longer. 'This is going to take a while. Maria will show you to your room.'

CHAPTER FIVE

CHANTAL watched as he walked away from her, hating herself for feeling regret at his departure. What was it about him that was so irresistibly attractive? He was breathtakingly handsome, of course, but it couldn't be just that, could it? Perhaps it was his strength—that aura of power that clung to him—or perhaps it was something else entirely.

It didn't really matter. All that mattered was that she was helplessly, hopelessly attracted to him and it didn't make any difference that their relationship had been doomed from the start.

Their mutual desire was awkward, she admitted silently, finally turning her head and studying the still, glass-like surface of the pool. Confusing. He didn't want to feel it because Isabelle clearly wasn't the sort of woman who drew his admiration. She didn't want to feel it because he wasn't the sort of man she could ever get involved with.

Suddenly aware that Maria was waiting patiently to escort her into the villa, Chantal rose quickly and followed her down a different path and into a fabulous bedroom suite that opened directly onto the pool terrace. It was light and airy, decorated entirely in white, and brightened by touches of deep blue. Colourful oil paintings adorned the walls and a large rug softened the floor. It was tasteful and understated, and as she glanced through an open door into a spacious, marble bathroom Chantal tried not to look over-awed.

If this was a guest bedroom, she couldn't begin to imagine what the master suite was like—and if Angelos Zouvelekis thought this was living 'simply' then she could only feel relieved that she wouldn't be exposed to any of the other aspects of his life.

But she already knew that their lives were as different as it was possible to be. He had wealth and he had family. She had neither. And as for possessions—

She turned and glanced at her one small case, which now stood in the middle of the room. It was a forlorn reminder of the fundamental differences in their lives.

What was she doing here?

Maria was watching her, her expression sympathetic, as if she sensed Chantal's growing misery.

'I will help you unpack,' she volunteered, but Chantal shook her head vigorously, her face burning with embarrassment at the thought of this woman seeing her lack of belongings.

She waited for Maria to leave, then opened the case herself and stared at the few outfits she'd brought with her.

Two dresses, a skirt, a pair of shorts, a few cheap tops and a swimming costume.

That was it. Nothing glamorous. Nothing that suited a few hedonistic weeks with a billionaire.

She didn't belong here.

What arrogance had made her think her presence would have any effect on his father's recovery? It was inevitable that Costas Zouvelekis would discover that their relationship wasn't real and once he discovered the truth everything would be worse.

She should never have come.

And she should never have used that ticket to the ball.

Pretending was one thing; actually trying to live a life that wasn't hers was dangerous and delusional.

But what could she do? For the time being, at least, she was trapped here and she had to make the best of it.

She fingered one of the dresses, wondering whether she could adapt it in some way. Or perhaps she didn't need to. Angelos had said that there was no dressing up on the island, so hopefully what she'd brought with her would be fine. She just had a sinking feeling that her idea of simple and his weren't going to coincide.

Hot and uncomfortable after her journey, she was just contemplating a shower when a faint breeze blew through the window. Walking across to the open doors, Chantal stared at the pool glistening in the afternoon sunlight. The water looked cool and inviting, and she couldn't think of a reason why she shouldn't swim.

Angelos was working and Costas was resting, so no one would be watching her. And by the time Angelos returned from making his next million she would be back in her room.

In fact, if she was very clever, it might be possible to avoid him for the entire fortnight. If Angelos worked during the day then their paths would only cross at mealtimes.

Angelos completed the last of his phone calls and ran a hand over his face in mounting frustration.

It was clear that his presence was needed in Athens. Ordinarily he would have taken a helicopter back to the city for a few days, but he didn't feel comfortable leaving until he was satisfied that his father was making a good recovery. Nor did he want to leave the older man with a woman less than half his age—especially when the woman in question fulfilled his father's definition of female perfection and was known to favour older men.

Just thinking about her made his stress levels soar to dangerous heights and he rose to his feet with a soft curse, rolling his shoulders to relieve the tension that had been mounting since he'd picked her up from the streets of Paris.

His body was humming with unfulfilled desire and he suppressed it ruthlessly.

What he needed was exercise: a hard, demanding physical workout that would use up some of his excess energy and take his mind off his ravenous libido. A hundred laps of the pool would be nowhere near as mentally and physically invigorating as truly satisfying sex, but it was the only thing on offer so it would have to do.

He flicked off the computer, found a pair of swimming shorts and strolled out onto the terrace, flexing the muscles of his shoulders in readiness.

So focused was he on his own needs that he felt a flare of irritation when he heard a soft splash coming from the pool and realised that someone else had shared his idea.

It couldn't be his father, because he was resting, which meant that it could only be the one person he'd been hoping to avoid.

His first reaction was to acknowledge that she was a remarkably good swimmer. Accustomed to women who preferred to pose by the edge of the pool rather than actually expose themselves to the realities of getting wet, he watched for a moment, surprised by her skill. She slid through the water with the fluid grace of a sea creature and Angelos was gripped by an attack of lust so powerful that it shocked him.

Also accustomed to being with women whose choice of swimwear could only be described as minimal, he couldn't immediately understand why a plain black swimming costume, clearly designed for sport rather than seduction, could have had such a powerful effect on him. A few minutes of studied concentration gave him the answer. His reaction had nothing to do with the swimming costume itself and everything to do with the woman wearing it.

The costume moulded to her shapely body, emphasising her long, slender legs, the tempting curve of her hips and her astonishingly small waist. Her body was incredible, and a rush of red-hot lust engulfed him. His reaction to her was so absolutely primitive that he took a step backwards, seriously disconcerted by the almost overpowering response of his body. He was *not* a man who indulged in thoughtless, mindless sex. Not since his teenage years had impulse played any part in his relationships.

It was true that beautiful women played an extremely important part in his life, but he was fiercely exacting in his choice and he was *always* the one in control. He made the rules. Relationships began and ended when he decided they should begin and end.

Understanding the true meaning of the word *temptation* for the first time in his life, Angelos inhaled deeply and attempted to obliterate thoughts that were as inappropriate as they were unwelcome. But his head was filled with a disturbingly clear image of her lush breasts trapped against his body and those long, long legs wrapped around his waist.

After the stress of the past two weeks, all he wanted to do was drag her out of the pool, strip her naked, and slake his lust in a vigorous session of mindless sex designed to leave them both numb and exhausted. At that precise moment he didn't actually *care* that she represented everything he despised in a woman. He'd even stopped caring that she'd ripped off two vulnerable men. How could that possibly affect him? *Vulnerable* wasn't a word that appeared in his vocabulary, so he wasn't in the least bit worried for himself. He was as tough and uncompromising as she was and all that interested him was a thorough exploration of the physical connection that drew them together.

Trapped in a vortex of sexual hunger, he suddenly acknowledged a more immediate problem.

Once she finished the lap and saw him, she'd also see the very visible outwards signs of his reaction to her.

Solving the problem with his customary decisiveness, Angelos strode to the edge of the pool and executed a perfect dive, plunging head-first into the deep end and allowing the cool water to close around his thoroughly overheated body.

He rose to the surface and then powered through the water in a perfect crawl, reaching the side just as she turned.

He saw from the shock in her eyes that she hadn't been aware of his presence until that moment.

'I didn't know anyone was—I thought you were working—' The water clung to her cheeks and her upper lip, and her dark eyelashes were fused into spikes. Far from attempting to keep her hair dry and away from the vicious attack of the pool chemicals, she'd obviously swum under the water and it now lay sleek and smooth against her head. Wet, it was darker than its usual shade, but her eyes still sparkled the same miraculous blue.

Disconcerted by the feeling that this whole situation was slowly spiralling out of control, Angelos dragged his eyes away from the tempting fullness of her mouth. *The cold water was supposed to have helped.*

'I needed some exercise.' Suddenly he wished he'd chosen a run on the beach as an alternative to the swim. It would have been hot, but he doubted that it was possible to be any hotter than he was at the moment. His entire body felt as though someone had lit a furnace inside it.

How was it possible to feel hot in cold water?

'Did you finish your business?' It was an innocent enough question, but sufficient to remind him of the stress he'd been trying to put out of his mind.

'For now.' Deciding that lingering next to her was putting unacceptable pressure on his self-control, Angelos terminated the conversation by plunging forward and swimming twenty lengths in rapid succession, pushing his body to the limits as he chose athletic endeavour as a means to work off some of his mounting tension.

He finished yet another length, and turned, but this time his body collided with something soft and yielding.

She gave a soft gasp and swallowed a mouthful of water as she sank below the surface of the pool.

'*Theos mou*—' Angelos immediately hauled her back to the surface, his hands sliding round her waist to support her as she choked and coughed. In the water she was slippery and lithe, and she rested her hands on his shoulders as she regained her breath. His fingers felt the smoothness of her skin and the surprising delicacy of her frame. He'd just decided that touching her had been a mistake of monumental proportions, when she looked at him. The light in her eyes changed from a sparkle of blue to a deeper shade and Angelos suddenly wanted her more than he'd ever wanted anyone in his life before.

Without thinking, he lowered his head and kissed her. Instantly her mouth opened in response to the demands of his. He probed with his tongue and the hot, sweet flavour of her mouth sent fire spurting through his veins. His fingers tightened on her waist and he pulled her hard against him, feeling her lithe, sinuous body twine itself around the hard length of his like a delicate flower seeking support and strength. She pressed herself against him, clearly as hungry for him as he was for her, and the last desperate flicker of self-restraint died inside him.

He was immersed in her—the scent of her, the feel of her, the race of her heart against his seeking hands—and his physical arousal was so powerful that it obliterated all other thought.

The water of the pool lapped quietly around them, and his kiss changed from exploratory to hard and savagely urgent. Fantasy merged with reality as her legs wound themselves around his waist and he felt her feminine mound press against him. He slid her costume from her shoulders. Her nipples were hard against his chest, physical evidence that her degree of desperation was no less than his. His hands swift and skilled, he tugged her costume down her legs. She unwound herself from him for long enough to free herself of the wet cloth, and then she was pressing against him again, and this time it was her hands that were doing the exploring.

Angelos felt her seeking fingers close around him. Light exploded in his head and a desperate urgency consumed him. The entire focus of his world became this one moment. *This one woman.*

Pumped up, and more aroused than he'd ever been in his life before, he closed his hands over the top of her thighs, driven by an almost primal need for satisfaction. In the water she was weightless, and she writhed and moved against him as she searched instinctively for the ultimate connection. Taking control, Angelos dug his fingers into her soft flesh and angled himself slightly until the tip of his erection finally met the burning heat of her damp core. The contact drew a gasp from her lips, and for a moment they remained poised on the very edge of the final intimacy. Then Angelos could wait no more. He entered her with a smooth, expert thrust and drove himself full length into her soft, quivering body.

She was exquisitely, maddeningly tight, and as her moist feminine heat closed around him his world imploded. Dimly he registered the sudden tension in her body, and felt a sharp pain in his shoulders as she dug her nails into hard muscle. His brain tried desperately to decipher the signals, but she was hot, so unbearably, deliciously hot after the cold of the water, that it took him a moment to clear his head sufficiently and register that something wasn't as he'd expected. He tried to control his own reaction, but at that moment her vice-like grip on his shoulders eased and she slid her arms round his neck, drawing closer to him as she moved her hips and pressed herself to him, urging him on.

Her soft moans of excitement drove him over the edge and his mind emptied. Blind to everything except the lure of immediate pleasure, Angelos surged into her again and again, losing himself in her soft heat, his usual self-control entirely absent, obliterated by a degree of sensation so overwhelming that it fell outside even his experience.

He felt her sudden gasp of disbelief, felt her body tremble against his, and then she shot into a climax so intense that the aftershocks ripped through his failing control. His own excitement amplified by her abandoned, extravagant response, he ground into her one more time before his body erupted and agonising pleasure transported him into a different stratosphere.

Angelos recovered first and, despite the unusually slow workings of his brain, realised that he had to do something with the limp, satiated woman who was currently clinging to him, her arms around his neck, her head buried in his shoulder.

Although they were shielded to some extent by the lush foliage that crowded and coloured the terrace, it was still an extremely public place.

What the hell had they both been thinking?

And then he realised that neither of them had been thinking at all. If he *had* been thinking then he wouldn't have chosen the swimming pool as a venue for an erotic encounter with a woman. The concept of sex as a spectator sport had never interested him and, given that sex was clearly an experience that was entirely new to her, he could only assume that she hadn't been thinking, either.

And that, of course, raised any number of questions.

But none of them could be voiced at this particular moment.

His stunned reaction to the realisation that she had been a virgin was eclipsed by the more immediate need to return her exquisite body to the swimming costume before someone walked onto the terrace and saw her naked.

Discovering that his skills at dressing a woman were by no means as well developed as his skills at *undressing*, Angelos slid a hand down her leg and attempted to ease her back into the costume. Despite marshalling all his powers of concentration, her full, creamy breasts were temptingly close and his movements were hindered by the fact that she flopped limp and unresisting in his arms.

'We *have* to get you dressed,' he breathed with exasperation, finally sliding the costume as far as her waist and then lifting her away from him in order to tackle the arms.

She was as limp as a rag doll, and when her eyes finally lifted to his she appeared to have difficulty focusing. With a soft curse he yanked at the straps of her costume and slid them over her arms until her body was finally covered.

Having achieved that first objective, Angelos lifted one of her hands and placed it on the side of the pool, so that she could support herself in the water. Then he stepped back from her, consciously placing distance between them. '*Talk* to me.'

His sharp command was met by dazed silence. She was looking at him as though he was from another planet, and he knew the feeling because he'd never felt so disconnected from reality in his life. Finally her lips moved, but no sound emerged. She appeared to be having difficulty forming words.

Against his will, his eyes were drawn to the softness of her mouth and he felt his body stir again. Perplexed and infuriated by the effect she was having on him, he stepped forward again, put his hands on her waist and lifted her bodily out of the water. It was clear to him that if there was any hope of a conversation it wouldn't be with both of them half naked in the pool—and anyway, the cold water was proving to be a remarkably ineffective libido-dampener.

Having lifted her clear of the water, Angelos placed his hands on the side and the muscles bunched in his shoulders as he levered himself upwards and sprang from the pool.

Water streaming off his body, he prowled over to the nearest sun lounger and reached for a towel. Securing it firmly around his waist, he took several deep breaths. Only then, when he was confident that he was back in control, did he turn to face her.

She hadn't moved.

She was still seated on the side of the pool, where he'd left her, like a doll whose body wasn't capable of independent movement.

With a soft curse he strode over to her, hauled her to her feet and wrapped a towel around her shivering frame with business-like efficiency. Then he pushed her into the nearest chair, his mind returning to its usual state of focus now that she was covered. 'Start talking.'

Talking?

He wanted her to speak about what had just happened?

Feeling dazed, and slightly removed from what was happening around her, Chantal stared at him blankly.

She had no idea what she was supposed to say. For her it had been—

She gave up trying to find the words. What exactly did he want to hear? That she was now a different person from the one she'd been yesterday? That it had surpassed her wildest dreams? *That she could have happily stayed in that pool with him for the rest of her life?*

Her gaze slid to his, but the contact was too much, *too intimate*, and she looked away immediately. But not before a disturbing image of him half naked had been imprinted on her brain. He was a vision of masculine power, with water glistening on his powerful torso, his eyes disturbingly intent as they rested on her face.

And *still* she couldn't speak—because the words were all jammed together in her head and she had no idea how to articulate the fact that *everything* felt different now.

Why didn't *he* say something? Or was he pretending that it hadn't happened?

She was just contemplating that disturbing possibility when she saw his mouth tighten.

How did he manage to look businesslike and intimidating, wearing just a towel?

'*Speak* to me,' he demanded, and his sharp tone finally roused her from her semi-conscious state.

'It was amazing,' she said faintly. 'You're very good.'

Shock flared in his dark eyes and he muttered something in Greek under his breath. 'That is *not* what I was asking you,' he breathed, faint colour highlighting the perfection of his bone structure. 'Let's do this another way. I'll ask the questions. You answer. Obviously you're *not* Isabelle Ducat.'

Realising that she'd just embarrassed herself, Chantal coloured deeply and shrank deeper inside the towel.

She'd just *assumed* that he'd wanted to talk about the sex because, for her, no other issues existed. What they'd just shared had driven everything else from her head. But obviously he wasn't similarly afflicted. For him there were issues much, much more important than talking about the sex. *Like her identity*.

Buying herself a little more time, she cleared her throat and tried avoidance tactics. 'What makes you think I'm not Isabelle Ducat?'

'Because the list of Isabelle's previous lovers reads like a telephone directory,' Angelos informed her helpfully. 'Whereas I now know that your list contains only one name. Mine.'

His blunt reminder of the intimacy they'd just shared caused the colour in her cheeks to deepen still further. Wriggling like a fish on a hook, she breathed deeply and told herself that he couldn't absolutely *know*. Could he? 'I don't see how you—'

'Don't even go there,' he warned in a soft voice. 'Unless you want me to treble your blushes by describing in meticulous detail exactly *how* I know.'

She breathed in and out and concentrated on a point between his feet and his knees. 'Oh.'

'Look at me,' he demanded, and she shrank slightly lower in her seat.

She couldn't look at him. It was just too, *too* embarrassing.

He sighed heavily. '*Please* will you look at me?' This time his voice was slightly less autocratic, as if he knew that he wasn't going to achieve his objective by sheer force alone.

Reluctantly, she looked. 'What do you want to know?'

'Start with who you really are.'

Who was she?

She wasn't sure she knew any more. She certainly didn't feel anything like the person she'd been half an hour previously.

Would her body ever feel the same again? 'I'm not Isabelle.'

'I *know* that.' His wide, sensuous mouth compressed as he struggled to contain his volatile nature. 'What I *don't* know is who you are and why you took her identity.'

'I didn't take her identity. Not really. You were the one who thought I was Isabelle.'

'You were in possession of her ticket.'

'Which just goes to show that external appearances can be deceptive.'

'The only deception around here was *yours*.'

Sensing a dangerous tension in him, Chantal felt her heart bump against her chest. 'It's true that I used the ticket, but I didn't pose as her. I didn't once use her name, and you weren't supposed to see the ticket.'

'This conversation is going round in circles and you are making *no* sense. How did you obtain the ticket in the first place?'

It was like being on the witness stand, being cross-examined by a very unsympathetic prosecutor.

What would he say, she wondered, when he discovered that the truth was even worse than the lie? 'It's a long story.'

'Give me the short version,' he ordered in a tense voice. 'I'm a guy who likes to get straight to the point, and we've already taken the long route. Let's try it from a different direction. How do you know Isabelle?'

'I *don't* know her. I met her in the hotel where she was staying.' Unable to look at him, Chantal examined each strand of the soft fluffy towel that now enveloped her. 'I was—' *oh hell* '—I was cleaning her room.'

There.

She'd said it.

Bracing herself for his reaction to her shocking confession, she sat there waiting, her fingers coiled in the damp folds of the towel.

Angelos said nothing.

Clearly he was so appalled that he'd flown a *cleaner* out to his island on his private jet that he couldn't even find the words to express his disgust. She gave a tiny shrug and tried to ignore the pain that tore at her insides.

'It's all right.' She tried to sound dismissive. Casual. 'Go ahead and say what's on your mind.' After all, she was used to it. *Used to being judged and instantly dismissed.* Struggling to close her armour around her. She lifted her eyes to his and she found him watching her from beneath thick dark lashes that concealed his expression.

'I'm still waiting for you to explain how you came to have the ticket.' He spoke with exaggerated patience. 'I'm assuming that if I wait long enough you will get to the point in the end.'

'I've reached the point.'

He rubbed his fingers over his forehead, as if to ease the tension. 'Chantal—that is your name, isn't it?' He spoke slowly and softly, as if he were hanging onto control by a thread. 'I'm not a very patient man. If a member of my staff had taken as long to tell me something as you have, I would have fired them by now.'

She stiffened defensively. 'I just told you I was working as a cleaner.'

'I heard you. At the moment I'm not interested in your career choice. What I'm still waiting to hear is how you came by the ticket.'

'But—'

'I'm *not* good with long, involved stories,' he informed her, his tone exasperated. 'Get to the point, *please,* before we both age any further.'

Chantal opened her mouth to say that she'd thought that the fact she was actually a cleaner *was* the point, but the burning impatience in his eyes made her think twice. Obviously he wanted more. 'I was cleaning her room. She was having a complete tantrum about what she should wear—flinging clothes all over the place and expecting me to pick them up. I thought she needed help, so I told her which dress I thought suited her best, and she just exploded in a rage. What did someone like *me* know about how to dress for an event like that? What did *I* know about attracting a rich man? I suffered fifteen minutes of verbal abuse, and then she decided that she wasn't going at all. So she flung her ticket in the bin and checked out of the hotel. I think she left Paris that same afternoon.'

'So you took the ticket out of her bin?' He condensed her lengthy confession into a few very blunt words.

'It sounds bad, I know. But—'

'—But you wanted to prove her wrong about not being able to attract a rich man?'

Affronted, Chantal glared at him. 'Of course not! It was nothing to do with attracting a rich man. It was a confidence thing.' She subsided in her seat. 'She made me feel *so* small— as if I were a completely different species to her.' She could have told him the rest of her story, of course, but there was no way she was doing that, when she'd already told him far, far too much about herself. As far as she was concerned she'd given him everything he was having. The rest was staying locked inside. She straightened her shoulders. 'And that's why I took the ticket. It wasn't about meeting men. I needed to prove to myself that she was wrong about me. Just for one night I wanted to dress up and be in her world.'

'You borrowed one of her dresses?'

'Don't be ridiculous. I would never have fitted into one of her dresses—and anyway, I wouldn't have done something like that. I made my own dress.'

'In the space of a few hours?'

Stung by his disbelieving tone, Chantal frowned at him. 'I'm good at sewing.' She'd had to be. It was the only way she could afford to dress the way she wanted to dress.

'So you turned up at the ball, like Cinderella, just to prove to her that she was wrong?'

'It wasn't about her at all. It was about me. I was proving it to myself. She made me feel—' The confession sat like a leaden lump in her mouth. 'She made me feel worthless. *Less* than her. I wanted to prove to myself that the people at the ball were just people. That I could mix and mingle in that world.' It wasn't the whole truth, but it was all he was getting from her.

'So that explains the bizarre conversation we had on the night of the ball when you wouldn't tell me who you were,' he muttered. '*Finally* I understand all that rambling about stereo- types and people not judging other people.'

'That's what they do,' Chantal said simply. 'People judge all the time, based on a number of superficial factors and their judgements are almost always wrong.'

'I don't suppose it occurred to you to tell me the truth?'

'You're joking! Of course not. You would have had me thrown out. And anyway, you were *furious* when you saw I'd been talking to your father.'

'Not because you were talking to him, but because you gave him the impression that we were seriously in love. The fact that you are here today is purely a result of the lies you told that night.'

She stared at him numbly. The warmth and passion they'd shared only moments ago had gone. 'I sat next to your father because he was the only friendly face in the place. I didn't know who he was. I didn't know who *you* were. And then he and I started to talk and—'

'And?'

She was silent for a moment, unwilling to confess that her imagination had run away with her. She didn't want him to know the impact he'd had on her at their first meeting. 'It was just a misunderstanding,' she said lamely, and he muttered something in Greek under his breath.

'You let me carry on believing that you were Isabelle, despite having had ample opportunity to tell me the truth. And I suppose the reason for that is all too obvious.' His tone was suddenly cool. 'I was offering you an all-expenses-paid holiday on a Greek Island. No wonder you stayed silent.'

It was the worst thing he could have said to her.

'You think I came here for a free holiday? That's *not* what happened!' Deeply offended by his interpretation, she leaped out of her chair, clutching the towel like a shield. '*You* were the one who insisted that I came.'

'And you didn't resist.'

Her heart was pounding. 'I came because you led me to believe that it would make a difference to your father, and I care about him. He was very kind to me.'

'So you made this enormous sacrifice for a guy you'd met once?' He lifted an eyebrow. 'You were doing me a *favour* by agreeing to fly by private jet to a secluded island for a few weeks of relaxation?' He was tying her in knots and he knew it.

'I don't care what you believe. It's the truth. But you're obviously so cynical and suspicious of women's motives that you think there's only one possible interpretation. Maybe you should give all your money away. Then you'd know, wouldn't you?' Still smarting with indignation, she blinked rapidly to clear the tears that had sprung into her eyes. He wasn't worth crying over. No man was worth that. All she could do now was pick up the pieces and start again. And learn from her mistakes.

But first she needed to get out of here.

After what they'd just done she could no longer stay as his guest. It wasn't possible.

Before she could move, Maria appeared on the terrace, an apologetic look on her face. She said something in Greek to Angelos and he gave a low growl, almost vibrating with impatience at the interruption.

'*Theos mou*, not now—' He raked his fingers through his glossy hair and then cast a look at Chantal. 'I have been waiting for this phone call—the timing isn't good, but I have to take it. We'll finish this conversation later.'

Not if she had anything to do with it.

Still bruised by his total lack of sensitivity, she didn't respond. What was there to finish?

He'd made his feelings perfectly clear, and she really didn't want to listen to any more.

He thought she was some sort of cold-blooded gold-digger.

Wrung out with the emotion of it all, Chantal watched in silence as he strode across the terrace. He was as cool and in control as ever. There was no evidence to suggest that he was a man caught up in the middle of an emotional crisis. *Which was yet another fundamental difference between them,* she thought numbly, her eyes clinging hungrily to his broad, muscular shoulders until they disappeared from view along with the rest of him.

She still wasn't sure how the whole thing had happened, or *why* it had happened. All she knew was that she felt like a balloon that had been popped before the party started.

Apart from acknowledging her utter lack of experience, Angelos apparently hadn't given a second thought to what had happened in the pool.

And yet *she'd* been unable to think of anything else. Every time he'd fired a question at her, she'd just wanted to say, *'But what about the sex?'*

It had been the most shocking, exhilarating, explosive experience of her life, and having suddenly discovered the depth of her sexuality she could now barely focus on anything else. The memory of their encounter was so clear that it dominated her mind in full, glorious Technicolor and her body ached in a way that was deliciously unfamiliar.

All the way through their conversation she'd just wanted him to stop talking, take her in his arms and do it all over again. Because she'd truly believed that what they'd shared had been unique and infinitely special.

And that was why she'd done it, of course. Because it had felt absolutely right. For the first time in her life she hadn't even stopped to question what she was doing.

But it hadn't been special for him, had it?

It hadn't even been worthy of comment. To him it had just been sex. And not just sex, but sex that obviously wasn't even worth remarking on. Disappointing sex. In fact, judging from his reaction, the whole episode had obviously been an entirely forgettable experience—nothing more than an exercise session for him—while the verbal exchange that had followed had possessed all the warmth and intimacy of a business meeting.

She cringed as she forced herself to face the truth.

He hadn't been able to get her out of the pool fast enough, had he?

She'd been ready to wind her arms round his neck and start it all again, but he'd lifted her out and plonked her on the side, clearly *not* sharing her desire for a repeat performance.

Obviously, as a woman, you couldn't win, she thought gloomily. Too much experience, like Isabelle, made you a slut. Too little made you boring.

Alone on the terrace, she released her death grip on the towel and allowed it to slide to the floor. Her costume had almost dried in the heat, and she ran a finger over her thigh, wondering if her body felt different on the outside—because it certainly felt different on the inside.

For the first time in her life she'd discovered what it was like to completely lose control, and the feeling was exciting and terrifying at the same time.

Uncomfortable thoughts from her childhood drifted into her head but she pushed them away again instantly, just not able to go there at this moment.

One thing she *did* know was that the sex had changed everything. She'd agreed to accept his hospitality only because he'd convinced her that his father's recovery depended on her presence. She'd been comfortable with it because there had been nothing personal in the invitation.

But now everything had changed.

And it was perfectly obvious what she had to do.

CHAPTER SIX

SERIOUSLY distracted, Angelos took his business call, snapped the head off the person on the other end of the phone and then instructed his PA in Athens not to put through any more calls.

At that moment he wasn't interested in talking to his senior management team. Nor was he interested in talking to any of the businessmen who clamoured for his attention on an almost hourly basis.

There were urgent matters demanding his attention. But for the first time in his life he didn't even care.

He should have been thinking about work, but all he could think about was sex.

Sex with Chantal.

Cursing softly in Greek, he paced the length of his office. His entire body was burning and unfulfilled and all he wanted to do was stride back onto the terrace, drag her somewhere extremely private and indulge in a repeat performance—complete with several encores.

Never in his life had he been so hot for a woman, and he didn't understand it because she possessed none of the qualities that he admired.

True, she was beautiful, but she was also dishonest—and she'd admitted as such. All right, so she wasn't Isabelle Ducat. She'd hadn't chosen to make a living out of divorce. But she *had* taken a ticket that wasn't hers, and she hadn't corrected him when he'd assumed her to be the owner of the ticket.

She'd posed as someone else, apparently more than comfortable to perpetrate that particular untruth. That fact alone should have been the sexual equivalent of sitting in a bath of ice cubes, because he *hated* deception.

He might have felt more kindly towards her had she just admitted that a few weeks in Greece with a billionaire had sounded like fun. Instead of which she'd insisted that she'd agreed to accompany him out of concern for his father.

So why, knowing all that, was his libido raging madly out of control?

Why did he feel like a teenager whose hormones were well and truly in control?

With a humourless laugh he forced himself to accept the obvious.

Because the sex had been nothing short of stupendous. That was why.

Deceitful she might be, but she'd also been a virgin, and the fact that he was her first lover had given him an incredible buzz.

Which meant that clearly he wasn't as modern in his attitudes as he liked to think.

He narrowed his eyes and ran through the facts logically.

All right, so she hadn't told him the truth. But she was right that he was the one who had insisted that she come. And, had she told him the truth about her identity, would it have changed anything?

No. He still would have wanted her to come for the sake of his father.

So what difference did any of it make?

She was here now, wasn't she?

The chemistry between them was amazing.

What was the problem?

She was here for a free holiday with a billionaire, so why not give her that holiday? And if it cost him a few dresses and the odd diamond necklace, so what?

They'd share incredible sex during the night, and during the day he'd arrange for her to spend as much time shopping as she could handle. She was using him for money, so why shouldn't he use her for sex?

Unable to concentrate, and deciding to abandon all further thoughts of work for the day, he strode into the suite of rooms that his father occupied when he was staying in the villa. 'How are you feeling?'

'Better by the hour.' Costas Zouvelekis was already dressed, ready for dinner. 'What did you do with your afternoon?'

Angelos stilled as erotic images flew into his brain. What had he done with his afternoon? *He'd had the most incredible sex of his life.*

In a public place.

He ran a hand over the back of his neck, seriously discomforted by the thought of what his father might have seen if he'd woken early from his rest and decided to relax by the pool. 'I worked.'

'Did you? Well, I hope you didn't leave Chantal on her own for too long. She's a woman worth guarding.'

'From whom? There is no one else here.'

'From boredom,' Costas said dryly, as he adjusted his shirt. 'When women become bored, they stray.'

Stray?

Angelos reflected silently on the fact that the last time he'd seen Chantal she'd been so shattered after his lovemaking that she hadn't seemed capable of moving her lips, let alone her legs.

'She isn't going to stray.' Why would she? He was in a position to give her the fantasy, and he had enough experience of her sex to know what she'd want. Jewels, dresses, handbags with strange names that were only available for a price, an unreasonable number of shoes, probably still more shoes—

He gave a faint smile. As long as he didn't have to be part of the selection process, he was more than happy to fund a seriously extravagant shopping spree.

Clearly she wasn't used to a life of luxury.

It would be fun to spoil her.

Never, ever become involved with a gorgeous Greek billionaire.

Having made herself sign off on that promise, Chantal snapped the suitcase shut and placed it on the floor. In the spacious, elegant room it looked laughably out of place.

Determined not to brood, she gave a little shrug and told herself that it didn't matter. The one good thing about having very few belongings was that it didn't take long to pack.

She was just about to reach for the phone and see if she could arrange for a car to take her to Athens when the bedroom door opened and Angelos strode into the room.

Clearly fresh from the shower, he'd changed into a pair of lightweight linen trousers and a shirt that emphasised his athletic physique. Tall and broad-shouldered, he emanated power and sexuality.

Her body leapt to life and she turned away, mortified that she was so susceptible to him. *Well, tough.* She was going to do what he was obviously doing and just not think about the sex. 'I was trying to arrange for a car. Now you're here, perhaps you could do it for me?'

'To go where, precisely?'

'Athens. I'll arrange a flight home from there.'

There was a tense silence. *'Home?'*

'Yes.' Summoning up as much dignity as she could, she reached into her bag and removed the roll of cash she'd counted out carefully a few minutes earlier. 'This is for you.' She thrust it into his hand and he stared at it in astonishment.

'What is this?'

'Money. You should know, since it obviously plays such an

important part in your life.' It was all the money she had; minus the amount she was going to need for her flight home. 'You can put that towards what I've cost you so far. Whatever you may think, I *don't* want a free holiday. I never should have come. I see that now. It's inevitable that a man like you would think that my reasons for coming here have something to do with money. In the circumstances, I don't even blame you for thinking that.' Some of her pride salvaged, she stepped forward and picked up the case, avoiding eye contact. It was terribly, terribly important that she didn't look at him. If she looked, she was lost.

'I don't want your money.' He dropped the money unceremoniously onto the nearest hard surface and Chantal tried not to flinch as she remembered just how long it had taken her to earn that amount.

'Well, I want you to have it. In fact, I insist.'

He glanced at the roll of notes and then back at her. 'Obviously my comments upset you,' he breathed. 'But you have to admit that I had cause.'

'Of course. Why else would someone like me be with someone like you?'

His body tensed. 'You pretended to be Isabelle Ducat, and she is the queen of gold-diggers.'

'Maybe. But even when you knew that I wasn't Isabelle your assumption was that I'd just come along for a free holiday.' Still suffering from a serious assault on her pride, Chantal clutched her case. 'It's obvious that you've discovered the sort of person I really am, so there's no point in me staying. Please arrange for me to leave the island. Is there a water taxi you can call?'

'I have no intention of calling you a taxi.' His tone had a raw edge to it. 'Put the case down.'

'No.'

He inhaled deeply. 'I can see that I've *seriously* upset you—'

'What makes you think that?' Her tone flippant, she walked

towards the door. 'We gold diggers have very thick skins. It's part of the job description.'

With incredibly quick reflexes, he crossed the room and grabbed her. 'Tell me why you accepted my invitation.' He hauled her hard against him, and she gasped as the contact ignited a flash of excitement deep inside her.

'You already know why.' Desperately she tried to shut down her response. 'It seemed a perfect way to enjoy a free holiday in the sun.'

'So, if that is the case, then why are you leaving now?'

'Because what we did makes it impossible for me to stay.'

'You are saying that because your feelings are hurt.' His mouth was dangerously close to hers and the heat between them was mounting. 'I am willing to admit that I owe you an apology.'

'No, you don't. I don't blame you for what you thought. It was a perfectly reasonable assumption in the circumstances.' Desperate to get away before she made a fool of herself yet again, Chantal tried to wriggle out of his grasp. 'Why else would someone like me have accompanied you?'

He held her firm. 'Why did you?'

Swamped by an almost agonising sexual tension, her anger subsided. 'Because of your father,' she muttered. 'You persuaded me that I could make a difference to his recovery. He was so kind to me that night at the ball. No one has ever been that kind to me before. I was feeling really vulnerable and horribly out of place. Which just goes to show that Isabelle was right all along. I didn't fit in.'

'Why would you want to?' He looked genuinely perplexed. 'Individuality is to be celebrated.'

Spoken like a billionaire who didn't follow any of life's rules, she thought weakly, wishing she possessed just a fraction of his self belief. 'You need masses of confidence to be different. I stood out. I felt as though everyone was staring.'

'They *were* staring. Because of your dress.'

'Yes, the dress was a huge mistake.'

'The dress was amazing. Where did you find it?'

She concentrated on one of the buttons of his shirt. 'They were refurbishing one of the hotel rooms and I found some red lining material that they'd thrown away. I thought it would look perfect.'

A stunned silence followed her frank confession. 'Are you telling me that your red dress started life on the inside of a *curtain*?'

'A very expensive curtain.' She shrugged. 'Why are you looking so shocked? You just said that individuality is to be celebrated.'

His handsome face was a mask of incredulous disbelief and he released her. 'That night—' His voice not quite steady, he rubbed his fingers over the bridge of his nose. 'You really *didn't* have a clue who I was, did you?'

She tried not to feel disappointed that he'd let her go. 'Of course I didn't know who you were. Why would I?'

It took him a moment to answer. 'Women usually do.'

'The women *you* mix with do. But I'm not one of those. And I wouldn't want to be,' she said firmly. She knew far too much about that type of woman. 'I only spoke to you because you spoke to me first. I'd been standing there, wishing I'd never decided to go to the ball, and then there you were.' She swallowed as she remembered the sharp intensity of that moment. 'And you were—there was—something—'

Their eyes met for a moment and he frowned. 'If all that is true, and you genuinely came to the villa because of concern for my father's health, then why are you leaving now?'

Because she had to.

Her fingers tightened on the case and she looked away from him so that she wouldn't be tempted. 'Because everything has changed. You know I'm not Isabelle, and our relationship has become—' She broke off and searched for the right word. 'Become personal. It goes against my principles.'

'Our relationship is now *exactly* the way my father always wanted it to be so to leave now makes no sense. We've merely dropped the pretence. It actually makes the situation simpler, not more complicated.'

'Not to me. We had—' She broke off again and cleared her throat, trying not to mind that he was quite prepared to pretend that the sex had never happened. 'What we did changes things.'

'I don't see how.'

'You think I'm just leeching from you.'

He glanced briefly towards the roll of notes he'd so carelessly discarded. 'Is that why you gave me the money?'

'I'm giving you the money because I don't want you to pay for me. I've never taken money from a man in my life.'

'I haven't offered you money.'

'You're paying for me to be here. That amounts to the same thing. You think I'm a gold-digger.'

Amusement flickered in his dark eyes. 'Gold-diggers generally aren't innocent virgins, *agape mou*. You're obviously not quite as familiar with the job description as you think you are.'

She couldn't think of a suitable reply, so she stayed silent.

He sighed. 'You're *not* leaving.'

She wished she could put the whole episode behind her as easily as he clearly had. 'I have to.' For so many reasons. Preserving her sanity was one, but so was maintaining her self respect.

'Chantal.' There was a decisive tone to his voice, like a judge who was summing up. 'You claim that you came here because of my father—'

'I did.'

'Then why would you leave? My father's needs are as great as they ever were. Greater, in fact. Since you arrived he has talked of nothing else. He is looking forward to joining us at dinner tonight. Nothing has changed.'

Chantal chewed her lip.

For him, nothing had changed. She wished she felt similarly indifferent. 'Everything has changed.' Her eyes moved to his and then skidded away. 'We—'

'Yes,' he said softly, 'we did. And given that you were a virgin I'm assuming that you aren't protected by any form of contraception?'

Her heart stumbled.

Pregnant? It hadn't even occurred to her that she might become pregnant. For a moment she forgot he was standing there as she considered that possibility. After her own childhood she'd never thought that she'd—

'I'll take your silence as a no,' he drawled softly, and she was silent for a moment as she did some rapid calculations in her head.

'It will be fine,' she muttered finally, her cheeks blossoming with colour because this was one topic she wasn't used to discussing with a man. 'So you don't need to think what you're thinking.'

'What am I thinking?'

'That I've set the ultimate honey trap.' She looked him in the eye, her expression fierce. 'Even if I *were* pregnant, I wouldn't take money from you.'

'Let's not argue about an issue which might never arise. The more pressing concern is what we do in the short term.'

'You're going to let me leave the island.'

His exasperated glance suggested that he wasn't used to people defying him. 'Whatever you may think of me, I'm not in the habit of indulging in careless sex regardless of the consequences.'

'So why did you with me?'

His dark eyes fastened on hers. 'I have been asking myself that same question for the past few hours. I'm sure the answer will come to me in time.'

She shrank as she imagined how much he must now be regretting his uncharacteristic lack of control. It was all too easy to imagine him calculating what that one awkward lapse was going to cost him in terms of money and adverse publicity. 'Well, anyway, it doesn't change the facts. I need to leave.'

'My father was kind to you.'

'Yes.'

'Then you must stay. You owe him this favour.'

She stared at him helplessly. 'That's not fair—'

'I don't play fair, Chantal,' he said softly. 'I play to win.'

She closed her eyes and tried to find the steely streak she needed to refuse. 'I can't—'

'His health is fragile. You have the ability to make him happy. Can you deprive him of that?'

She opened her eyes. 'You're totally ruthless, aren't you?'

'Focused.'

She turned her head away, feeling as though she were a leaf caught in a hurricane. The force of his personality was too powerful to resist.

'I don't see how my presence will really help him…' But she was wavering and he sensed it, moving in for the kill like a lion spotting a wonded antelope.

'Your presence could make all the difference to his recovery.'

She wanted to say no, but she couldn't forget the kindness his father had shown her.

'All right.' The words were dragged from her lips. 'I'll stay—'

'Of course you will.' Clearly supremely confident of his own negotiation skills, he didn't look surprised by her decision.

'—But only if you let me pay you.'

'I don't understand your desire to be independent.'

'It isn't about independence—' She broke off, realising that if she stuck by that claim then she'd have to explain herself. *And she had no intention of doing that.* He already knew far too much about her.

His dark eyes narrowed. 'I don't want your money.'

'Take it,' she said fiercely. 'Or I'm going home right now.'

He studied her in silence, his expression unreadable. 'All right. If it makes you happy.' With economy of movement he reached for the roll of notes and slipped it into his pocket. 'So, now that problem is solved you can unpack your suitcase. My father is waiting for us on the terrace. Why don't you change and then join us?'

It was only after he'd strode from the room that Chantal realised they *still* hadn't discussed what had happened in the pool.

'I'm not that hungry,' Costas protested as Chantal spooned a small helping of roasted peppers onto his plate.

'They're delicious,' she enthused. 'You just have to try them. Just a mouthful.'

'Women.' Costas sighed and picked up his fork. 'They never let a man rest.'

'You can rest later.' She helped herself to a different dish, examining the contents closely. 'What's this?'

'Fasoláda—kidney beans baked in the oven with vegetables, herbs and olive oil. It's delicious. Try it.'

'Only if you try some, too.' Her smile engaging, she spooned a small amount onto his plate and watched while he ate. 'Well?'

'It's good.'

Feeling like a spare part, Angelos watched as she cleverly coaxed his father to eat, selecting small quantities of healthy food for him to try.

Only when she was satisfied that he'd eaten something did she turn her attentions to her own plate. After several mouthfuls she smiled at his father. 'You're right, it *is* delicious. I'd swim through a shark-infested pond to eat this again.'

His father laughed with delight and reached for another dish. 'If you think that's good, then you should try this one—'

The two of them were like excited children and Angelos watched as his father flirted outrageously with Chantal.

Now that he knew she wasn't Isabelle Ducat, he was noticing things he should have noticed before. Like the fact that she didn't actually flirt. No simpering, no hair tossing, no lowered lashes. Nothing, in fact, that could be described as flirtatious. She just had an open, friendly attitude.

He remembered that night of the ball, and recalled that one of the things about her he'd found so attractive was that she'd been so different from everyone around her.

She'd shown a cheeky sense of humour, a playfulness that was quite different from flirting.

It was no wonder his father had *liked her.*

And no wonder that she was having such a powerful effect on him.

He'd never been so aware of a woman. The curve of her mouth when she smiled; the slight dimple at the corner of her mouth, the light that appeared in her eyes when she laughed.

And then there was her body... At that point he found his descriptive powers severely challenged. All he knew was that she appeared to have been designed specifically to distract a man from whatever path he was taking.

Suddenly he couldn't wait for dinner to end so that he could finish what they'd started in the pool.

Trying not to dwell on the fact that Angelos had barely spoken to her over dinner, Chantal stepped into the shower. In the end she'd left him on the terrace with his father, both of them engrossed in an unintelligible conversation about the Far Eastern money markets.

And now she stood under the sharp jets of water, satisfied that Costas had at least eaten something. She just needed to make sure that he did that at every mealtime.

Reaching for one of the fluffy towels that were piled in uniform rows, Chantal walked out of the shower and into the bedroom.

Angelos was sprawled on the bed, talking in rapid Greek into his mobile phone.

Shocked to see him there, she was about to retreat into the bathroom when he noticed her and ended the call with a decisive stab of one long finger. 'You were so long I was about to join you in the shower.'

'What are you doing in my bedroom?'

'*Our* bedroom, *agape mou*,' he drawled softly, extending a hand in her direction. 'Come to bed.'

She clutched the towel. 'What for?'

His eyes shimmered with amusement. 'I understand that you're inexperienced, but surely not *that* inexperienced.'

Chantal didn't move. 'You're suggesting that we share a bed?'

'Generally that's what happens.' Dark lashes veiled his expression and she felt her tummy jump like a grasshopper.

'But you—I—' She broke off. 'It was a one off.'

'I don't do "one-offs". I've already told you, casual affairs are not my style.'

'But that's ridiculous—we hardly know each other.'

'On the contrary. We *know* each other in the most literal and intimate sense of the word,' he drawled, and she felt the colour flood into her cheeks.

'That's different. Neither of us was thinking.'

'Sex doesn't generally require a great deal of intellectual input.'

Her heart was pounding against her chest. 'But you didn't even enjoy it,' she blurted out impulsively. 'You were really bored.'

'*Bored?*' Incredulous dark eyes swept her flushed cheeks. 'At what point, precisely, did I appear to be bored?'

'Afterwards—when you didn't once mention it.'

'I've always considered sex to be more of a practical than an academic subject. More about doing than talking.' His voice was deep and impossibly sexy. 'And at the time we had rather more pressing topics to discuss—such as your identity. Call me old-fashioned, but my preference is always to at least know the name of the person with whom I've been intimate.' He sprang off the bed and strolled towards her, a look of intent on his handsome face.

As his hand slid decisively around her wrist, her bones melted away like chocolate over a flame. 'Angelos—'

'I like the way you say my name,' he purred, sliding his other hand behind her neck and drawing her towards him. 'And for the next few hours that's the only word I want to hear from you. I'm tired of talking.'

She opened her mouth to give him all the reasons why she had no intention of doing this, but he was standing so close that a helpless rush of excitement engulfed her. It was like being in the path of a red-hot lava flow.

Her body was trembling with delicious anticipation and she gave a moan and swayed towards him. He brought his mouth down on hers and his powerful body urged her back towards the bed, his hand divesting her of the towel just seconds before she tumbled back onto the mattress.

He came down on top of her with single-minded intent, his heated gaze devouring every detail of her trembling naked body.

A frantic mixture of desperation and embarrassment, Chantal squirmed under his frank appraisal. *What if he didn't like what he saw?* 'Angelos—'

Clearly suffering none of the inhibitions she suffered, his eyes drifted back to hers and he lowered his head once again. 'You really are *incredibly* beautiful,' he groaned, and this time when he kissed her it was like dropping a burning match into a barrel of gunpowder. Her insides exploded in a shower of agonising sensation and she dug her nails into the firm muscle of his shoulders, so unbelievably aroused that she couldn't really grasp what was happening to her.

He controlled her utterly, completely sure of himself as he turned his attention to her breasts, using his fingers and his mouth with such erotic expertise that the heat inside her grew to hazardous levels.

She was burning. Every single inch of her body was sizzling and smouldering. She lifted her hips in frantic demand and expectation.

His fingers slid lower, skimming her abdomen and resting just short of this ultimate destination. The fact that he was still capable of control when she had none might have been humiliating, but she no longer cared. She was just too desperate to care.

'Am I the first man to touch you?' His husky demand penetrated her dazed brain.

'Yes, yes—' But he hadn't touched her yet, had he? And if he didn't do it soon she thought she might explode, because it wasn't possible to be any more aroused than she was at that moment. 'Angelos—please—'

He gave a satisfied smile and stripped off his boxer shorts. 'I have never wanted a woman as much as I want you. You're mine. Exclusively.' It was an unashamed statement of possession but she didn't even care.

Confronted by the breathtaking vision of Angelos naked, she felt her mouth dry and her excitement levels shoot higher still.

He was magnificent: his shoulders broad, his abdomen flat and as for the rest of him—

Reminding herself that they'd already done it once, and everything had fitted, Chantal gasped as she felt his hair-roughened thigh brush against her.

Why didn't he touch her?

What was he waiting for?

The ache inside her was almost painful and she arched against him, unconsciously begging for his touch, aware that he was torturing her on purpose.

At last his fingers moved, brushing through the soft curls that protected her soft, damp core. And then finally he touched her where she was longing to be touched, and his fingers were so impossibly sure and skilful that she immediately shot into an orgasm so intense that she couldn't breathe. Consumed by sensation, she sobbed his name—and then whimpered in disbelief as he pulled her beneath him and surged into her with propulsive force, taking her with long, hard strokes that launched her into the outer reaches of ecstasy.

Out of her mind with excitement, Chantal clutched at his shoulders, his primal possession starting up a chain reaction that was outside her control. Without having time to breathe or recover she was plunged straight into another orgasm, her body tightening around his, driving him to his own peak. The sudden increase in masculine thrust sent her over the edge yet again, so that this time they exploded together, both of them consumed by the same fire.

In the aftermath she lay shocked and stunned and he smoothed her hair away from her face with a surprisingly gentle hand. 'You are amazing—'

She was just about to point out that *he* was the one who had made it all happen when his fingers began another extremely intimate exploration.

With a moan of excitement and disbelief, she gazed at him in a state of helpless abandon. 'You can't mean to do it again—'

'You're *so* innocent. I love the fact that this is all new to you. You have much to learn, *agape mou*,' he said huskily, 'and I am delighted to be the one to teach you.'

CHAPTER SEVEN

CHANTAL woke to find the bed empty and no sign of Angelos.

Even without glancing at her watch she knew it was late.

Hot sun shone through the open bedroom doors, illuminating the room like a stage set, and from outside by the pool she could hear the low hum of male voices.

Obviously the physical demands of the night and the complete absence of sleep hadn't affected him at all.

Memories flooded back into her head with embarrassing clarity.

It had been like being caught in the focus of an earthquake, watching helplessly as everything familiar had crumbled around her. She'd had no control over her reactions. *She hadn't recognised herself.*

Covering her face with her hands, she gave a groan of disbelief as she forced herself to face the uncomfortable truth.

She had made love with a man she barely knew. Again and again. And then again.

And not just any man. A man with more wealth than she could possibly imagine. A billionaire. Which made the situation a hundred times worse as far as she was concerned.

Hadn't she always promised herself that she would *never* have that sort of relationship? Not when she, of all people, knew what such a relationship meant.

She'd come here on her own terms, living by her own rules. And now everything had changed. Sex had shifted the balance. Instead of being a guest, she was—she was—

What was she? His mistress? His lover?

It didn't really matter what she called herself, because the reality was that technically she was now a kept woman. She was on *his* territory, living by *his* rules. *He was paying for her.* She was staying in his villa, eating his food, swimming in his pool, luxuriating in his bathroom—

Her breathing suddenly increased and she sat upright in bed, faintly panicky as the reality of her situation sank in.

She'd let a man buy her.

All right, he hadn't actually given her *cash*, but she was using his hospitality, which amounted to the same thing, and she couldn't allow that to carry on. Not for one moment did she fool herself into believing that the money she'd given him anywhere near covered their expenses so far.

Which meant that she *had* to leave.

How could she stay when staying went against everything she believed in? He wanted sex from her, that was all. Sex.

She became conscious of every delicious ache and tingle in her body and she glanced at the rumpled sheets, admitting to herself that her reluctance to leave wasn't all to do with his father.

She was crazy about Angelos.

What woman wouldn't be?

But it wasn't an equal relationship, was it? And she'd always promised herself that this wasn't going to happen to her.

Angelos had drained his third cup of coffee and was trying to concentrate on what his father was saying when Chantal stepped hesitantly onto the terrace.

No one looking at her could have been in any doubt as to how she'd spent the previous night. Her eyes were adorably sleepy, her mouth was soft and bruised, and the haphazard way that her blonde hair had been pinned to the top of her head suggested that her hands hadn't been quite steady at the time.

The simple pair of shorts she'd elected to wear simply accentuated her ridiculously narrow waist and the generous curve of her hips. She somehow managed to ooze sexuality and innocence at the same time, and the combination was intoxicating.

His mind suddenly wiped of all coherent thought, Angelos endeavoured to recall exactly *why* he'd opted to join his father for breakfast when there had been such a good reason for staying in bed. Looking at her now, he cursed his generosity in allowing her to sleep, wishing instead that he'd woken her up and continued his exploration of her exquisite body with the benefit of full daylight.

Clearly her mind was running along the same lines as his because she met his gaze and her cheeks immediately turned a deep shade of rose. Her eyes slid longingly to his mouth and then she looked away again.

'I'm sorry I'm so late,' she mumbled, and Angelos watched with growing amusement, wondering whether she was aware that she'd as good as announced their level of intimacy to anyone watching.

He loved the fact that she couldn't hide her feelings.

At least his father would need no convincing as to the exact nature of their relationship, he thought with wry humour as he stood up and pulled out a chair for her.

She blushed more than any woman he'd ever met and he found it incredibly appealing.

'*Kalimera.*' His hand brushed against hers and he heard her softly indrawn breath. Then she sat quickly in the chair and the sudden flash of lush, creamy flesh and the glorious scent of her hair sent an explosion of lust tearing through his body. The desire to remove her clothing and rediscover her amazing and addictive curves was so powerful that Angelos inhaled sharply and stepped backwards.

Costas chuckled and put down his coffee cup. 'It's time I left the two of you alone.'

Realising that his reaction to her had clearly been as transparent as hers had been to him, Angelos frowned. 'Don't be ridiculous.'

What was the matter with him?

Discretion and discipline were just two of the rules he stringently applied to his love life, but so far both had been notably absent in his dealings with Chantal.

When he remembered the passionate interlude in the swimming pool, he felt as though he were reviewing the actions of a stranger.

His father's smile widened. 'You should congratulate yourself, Chantal,' he said cheerfully, reaching for another piece of fruit. 'You've achieved what other women have only dreamed of achieving. You've distracted my son from the share price. This is the first meal I've shared with him when he hasn't bored me to death on the subject of the money markets. In fact, he hasn't noticed me since he sat down at the table. Clearly he has something far more absorbing on his mind.'

Wishing he'd encouraged his father to leave them alone, Angelos ignored the growing sexual hunger inside him and instead applied cold, hard logic to the situation. What would he normally be doing after a night of incredible sex?

The answer was that *he* would be working, having left the woman in his life to occupy herself in whatever way she found most amusing. In his experience, that usually involved shops.

And that, of course, was exactly what he should do in this case. Send her shopping. It would remove the distraction caused by having her around, enable him to get some work done, and it would please her. And he *wanted* to please her.

Satisfied with that solution, Angelos lounged in his chair, a faint smile touching his sensuous mouth as he anticipated being on the receiving end of her gratitude that coming night.

'Contrary to my father's expectations, I do have to work today,' he said smoothly. 'You're welcome to occupy yourself around the villa, or Jannis can take you by boat to the mainland. We keep a car there, so if you fancy a trip of some sort. Shopping, perhaps?' He waited for her face to brighten with the appropriate display of enthusiasm, but she merely stared at him.

'Shopping for what? I don't need anything.'

'Then feel free to buy something you *don't* need,' Angelos drawled, extremely amused by her naïve response. He decided that he liked her more and more. She was original, and entirely different from the women he usually dated. 'The female desire to shop usually stems more from want than need.'

'There's nothing I want, either.'

Never before having found himself in the position of having to encourage a female to spend money, Angelos was momentarily at a loss as to how to respond. Then it occurred to him that she might be assuming that he was expecting her to pay for herself. 'I'm offering you my credit card, *agape mou.*'

Her narrow shoulders tensed. 'I don't want your credit card. I don't want anything from you.'

His father laughed with delight. 'A woman who doesn't want anything from you, Angelos. Take my advice and hold onto her.'

Angelos frowned. Was she playing a game? Was this all to do with his remark about gold-diggers? *Was she trying to impress him?* 'If you change you mind just speak to Jannis,' he said smoothly. 'He can take you anywhere you want to go.' But he was starting to wonder whether that should be the bedroom. If it weren't for the numerous business calls that were demanding his attention, he would drag her there right now, without even giving her time for breakfast.

Early night, he promised himself, his body tightening as he remembered how responsive she'd been the night before. 'Coffee?'

'Please.' She reached forward and lifted the pot, not waiting for Maria to serve her. Then she smiled at his father. 'How are you feeling?'

'Like a spring lamb. After breakfast I am starting some exercises with the physiotherapist.' He glanced at Angelos. 'You chose her. Is she better-looking than the nurses?'

'She's a grandmother,' Angelos said dryly as he lifted an orange from the bowl. 'And the purpose of her visit is to assist in your recovery, not liven up your love life.'

'I have no problems with a mature woman, but *is she thin*?'

Intercepting Chantal's surprised look, Angelos smiled. 'My father is very wary of thin women.' Deftly he peeled the orange and placed the segments on her plate. 'Try this. It's straight from the tree and absolutely delicious.'

His father waved a finger. 'It isn't natural for a woman to be thin. A thin woman—'

'—has her priorities all wrong,' Angelos finished, watching transfixed as Chantal licked her fingers of the last of the juice. Her lips were soft and pink, and as they closed round her fingers he felt the immediate and predictable response of his body. 'My father thinks a woman should enjoy her food.'

'When it tastes as good as this, it would be hard not to.' She reached for another segment of orange and then met his gaze. Her hand stilled.

Aware of the effect he'd had on her, Angelos smiled.

The anticipation was burning him up inside and clearly she felt the same way.

Driven by the demands of his libido, he was tempted once again to ignore the mounting pressures of his business—but then he reminded himself that the wait would be good for both of them. It would make the conclusion all the more satisfying.

By the time the sun set, both of them would be so desperate that the night ahead would prove to be doubly satisfying.

It was the perfect solution.

Why hadn't she thought of it immediately he'd suggested that she might like to go shopping?

As the boat sped across the bay, Chantal kept a close eye on the coastline.

When they arrived at the harbour, she leaned forward and spoke to Jannis. 'This is perfect. Can we stop here?'

He moored the boat. 'There are no expensive shops here. I will drive you to Athens.'

'I don't want expensive shops.' She stepped out of the boat and scanned the restaurants that were strung along the beach. 'This will do fine.'

'You wish to spend half an hour here?'

'No, I want to spend the day here.' Grabbing her bag, she smiled at him. 'Thank you so much for the lift. Is there a water taxi or anything that would take me back to the island?'

Jannis looked startled. 'No taxi—' He cleared his throat. 'If you give me a time, I would be honoured to collect you.'

Chantal wrinkled her nose and thought for a moment. She didn't really want him to collect her, but what alternative did she have? 'All right. If you're sure. Shall we say five o'clock?'

That should give her plenty of time to do what needed to be done.

Never had Angelos found so little in his working day to interest him.

After just one phone call he found himself staring at the door of his office, wondering what Chantal was doing.

Was she lying in the sun? Swimming?

The memory of her body outlined by a tight swimming costume sent the heat surging through his body and he ran a hand over the back of his neck, struggling against the impulse to go outside and check that she had everything she needed.

Concentration eluded him, and by the time Maria came to tell him that lunch was served on the terrace he'd already decided to take the rest of the day off and take Chantal back to bed. So it came as a shock to discover that she wasn't there.

'Jannis took her in the boat to the mainland,' Maria told him as she placed several dishes on the table. 'He's picking her up at five o'clock.'

She was planning to be out all day?

Angelos's expression didn't alter. *So much for her protests about not wanting or needing anything.*

Obviously that had all been for his benefit, he thought cynically as he picked an olive out of a bowl and silently examined its dark, glossy skin. As soon as he was out of the way she'd vanished on a shopping trip.

Which wasn't surprising.

What was surprising was how disappointed he felt.

Why should he be disappointed when she was simply doing what her sex was programmed to do?

Exhausted after a night without sleep and a day spent on her feet in the heat, Chantal lay on the sun lounger, sipping an iced drink and listening as Costas Zouvelekis entertained her with stories of Angelos as a child.

'—and he was so competitive. *Always* he had to win.' Costas gave a wry smile at the memory. 'If he found something difficult, then he just set his jaw and tried again until he succeeded.'

'I hope you're not showing her baby pictures.' A deep, dark drawl came from behind them, and Chantal turned and saw Angelos standing there, a sardonic expression in his eyes as he watched them.

He looked so sleek and handsome that her stomach dropped like an express elevator with a major technical fault.

Watching her reaction with an approving smile, Costas stood up. 'I'm going to have a short rest before dinner.'

Angelos watched him walk across the terrace and into the villa and then his gaze swivelled back to Chantal. 'I missed you today.' His eyes dropped to her mouth, and for a moment she couldn't breathe. Her body heated in an instantaneous response that shocked her. The attraction between them was so powerful that it obliterated everything else. And it didn't matter how much she tried to control it, she just wanted him *now*.

'You missed me?'

'Did you doubt it?' His voice was low and seductive and he sat down on the edge of her lounger. The width of his shoulders blocked out the sun, and for a moment she was in the shade unable to think of anything except the differences between them. *Her* legs were creamy and smooth. In contrast his thighs were strong and well muscled, shadowed by dark hairs that simply emphasised his masculinity. Male and female—the contrast between them increased the sexual heat still further.

'Did you work today?' She shifted her gaze from his legs to his face and then wished she hadn't because the dark stubble that hazed his jaw was just another indication of his virility.

'I tried to, but I confess my concentration was a little lacking.' His eyes were hooded, the sudden curve of his mouth slow and seductive. 'Are you tired?'

'Tired?'

'You had a long day—' with his customary assurance he ran a long, bronzed finger over her trembling thigh and lingered at the curve of her knee '—and you didn't have much sleep last night.'

'Last night?'

'You are supposed to answer me, *agape mou*,' he drawled softly, 'not just repeat everything I say like a parrot.' But the amusement in his eyes made it clear that he was well aware of the effect he was having on her, and the fact that he knew simply increased her embarrassment.

No wonder he had a healthy ego, Chantal thought faintly, *if all women were as useless at hiding their feelings as she was.*

She tried to think of something cool and dismissive to say, but he was just too close for her to concentrate on speech. The density of his eyelashes made his eyes seem even darker and for a moment she just gazed at him, enraptured by the lean perfection of his bone structure and his firm, sensuous mouth. He was extravagantly, impossibly handsome and it was impossible not to stare.

With a soft laugh he leaned forward, but stopped just short of kissing her, his mouth tantalisingly close to hers. 'If you won't talk,' he murmured softly, the words brushing her lips in a sensuous promise, 'then we will have to find some other way of communicating.'

Her excitement levels soaring through the roof, Chantal gave a low moan of desperation, the anticipation of his kiss so acute that it was like a physical pain. When he finally ended the torture and captured her mouth with his, the heat erupted between them in a violent explosion of sexual chemistry.

The passion threatened to soar out of control, but this time Angelo pulled back. '*Not* here.' His usually faultless accent was a long way short of perfect and his voice was hoarse. 'We will go inside.'

'No.' Seriously disturbed by how out of control she felt when he touched her, Chantal slid away from him.

'No?' It was his turn to repeat her words, and he did so in such a disbelieving tone that at any other time she would have smiled. But she was a long way from smiling. Her insides were suffering from a serious case of turbulence.

'No. We can't. Not until we've sorted something out. It's important.'

'Ah—' His gaze softened with understanding. 'You are talking about contraception, but you needn't worry. This time I promise to take very good care of you—as I did last night.'

'I'm not talking about contraception.' The fact that it hadn't even occurred to her was yet another indication of just how dangerously he affected her.

His gaze was indulgent. 'You want to show me your purchases?'

'What purchases?' Concentrating was impossible when everything about him made a woman want to touch: his glossy hair, his bronzed skin, the sheer masculinity of his athletic physique.

'You spent the day shopping,' he reminded her, his eyes amused. 'I'll tell Maria to make dinner an extra-special occasion, so that you can have an excuse to wear whatever it is that you bought.'

'I didn't buy anything.'

He lifted a brow in sardonic appraisal. 'You spent an entire day shopping and you didn't buy anything? How is that possible?'

'I wasn't shopping.' Deciding that the sooner they sorted everything out the sooner her principles would be satisfied, and they could do what they were both longing to do, Chantal dug her hand into her bag and pulled out an envelope. 'Here. This is for you.' She pushed it into his hand and he looked at her quizzically, before flipping open the envelope with a lean finger and examining the contents.

'Not again!' A flash of exasperation in his eyes, he fingered the notes and looked at her with a total lack of comprehension. 'Why are you giving me money this time?'

'It's for my food, expenses—w-whatever you want to call it,' Chantal stammered. 'And please don't argue, because I *really* want you to take it. Actually, I insist on it. I mean, when I was here because of your father it didn't matter so much because I was here for a reason. But now that we've had—now that our relationship has changed—and it's—I can't have sex without paying you…' Aware that her words were spilling out in the wrong order, she let her voice trail off. She waited for him to give a nod of understanding, but his only response was a long, incredulous silence.

Finally, after what seemed like ages, he spoke. 'You're *paying* me for sex?'

'No!' Flustered, she shook her head. 'Of *course* not.'

'You said that you can't have sex without paying me.'

'I didn't mean it the way it sounded.'

'But you're giving me money?'

'Because I don't want you subsidising me.'

'You are making *no* sense whatsoever.'

That was probably true. It was almost impossible to make sense or sound even vaguely coherent when he was sitting so close to her and the dark hairs on his thigh were brushing against the sensitive skin of her leg. He was everything male and all she could think of was— 'After what happened yesterday—last night—I have to pay you something towards my food.'

He dropped the envelope onto her lap. 'When you said that there was something important that we needed to talk about, I assumed you meant contraception.'

'This *is* important. If you don't take the money then I'll feel as though you're keeping me, and I don't want that.'

He stared at her. 'That's what most women dream about. Finding a rich man to indulge them.'

'Well, it isn't what *I* dream about. It isn't what I want and as far as I'm concerned the only way we can continue this relationship is if you let me pay for my keep.'

'Forget it.' His tone was clipped and the heated atmosphere cooled considerably. 'I don't want your money.'

'Why not?' Genuinely astonished by his reaction, it was her turn to stare. 'You *hate* it when women are only interested in you for your money.'

'But you're not interested in me for my money, are you?' He

rose to his feet with the effortless grace of a panther. 'You didn't even know who I was when we first met.'

'I know who you are now.'

'But any benefit you've derived from my wealth has been a by-product of our relationship, not the cause of it. There's a subtle distinction.'

'Is there? Well, it's too subtle for me to understand,' she mumbled. 'As far as I'm concerned I want to make a financial contribution. I *have* to. Why should you pay for what I'm eating? I don't understand your problem. It should make you feel good, knowing that I'm with you because I *want* to be with you, not because of the money or the lifestyle.' And it was necessary for her. *Dark feelings tangled with her newfound happiness.*

'Taking money from you would *not* make me feel good. If you want to know what will make me feel good then come with me now and I'll show you.' He reached out a hand and hauled her to her feet. As his arms came round her waist she turned her head away, using every drop of will power at her disposal.

'I can't do that.' The temptation to just turn her head and kiss him was agonising. 'Not if you won't let me pay anything towards the cost of staying here.' She could feel the warmth of his breath against her cheek and the friction of his body against hers: *hard muscle and rough male skin against her own soft flesh.*

'You're saying no? You're refusing me? You're pretending you don't want this?' His voice was a soft, masculine purr and she gave a low moan of denial as she felt the warm pressure of his hand against the bare flesh of her back. His lips brushed the corner of her mouth and her head swam and her eyes drifted shut.

'I'm saying no,' she whispered, 'unless you take the money. *Take* the money, Angelos.'

He muttered something in Greek and released her, tension visible in every muscle of his powerful frame. 'I will *not* let you pay.'

'If I don't pay,' she muttered, battling against a powerful desire to throw herself back into his arms and abandon her principles, 'then I'll have to go home.'

'You didn't seem to have a problem with the concept of accepting my hospitality when we were in Paris.'

'That was different. You wanted me to help your father. I was doing you a favour.'

'And I want you to do me several more favours,' he breathed, the exasperation in his eyes suddenly replaced by something much, much more dangerous. 'Come to bed and I will show you.'

'*Don't* tease me.'

'Why not? I love it when you blush.' He slid a finger under her chin, forcing her to look at him. 'I want you, and I want you *now*. And you want me, too. You are aching for me—aren't you?' His fingers moved purposefully down her body, his touch skilled and sure as he transformed her into a quivering wreck with just the stroke of his hand.

'You're not playing fair, Angelos—'

'*You* are the one who is not playing fair.' His hand lingered on the curve of her hip in a deliberately intimate caress. 'Imposing all these ridiculous rules on our relationship.'

'Just one rule,' she gasped, trying to ignore the seductive stroke of his fingers.

'You can stop this foolishness, *agape mou*. I'm suitably impressed. And none of that matters any more. All day I have been thinking about last night.'

'Impressed? What do you mean?'

'I'm impressed by your determination *not* to take my money. It's very refreshing. But there's no need to go over the top.'

'I'm not saying it to impress you,' she moaned, pushing against his chest. 'And you're not listening to me.'

'I'm listening. I just don't like what I'm hearing.'

'Do you always ignore things you don't like?'

'No.' He gave a casual shrug. 'I just turn them into things I do like. And *I* don't understand *your* problem. We are in a relationship and I am spoiling you. What's wrong with that?'

'Everything, if the spoiling is financial.' Desire sizzled between them and her struggle to ignore it seemed impossible.

He was clearly fighting the same battle. His gaze dropped to her mouth and lingered there. 'And what if I took you out to dinner? Would you insist on paying?'

'Of course I would.'

Incredulous dark eyes lifted to hers. 'You'd be pushing a pile of used euros into my hand at the end of the meal? Is that what you're saying?'

'Maybe. Gold credit cards aren't the only way to pay, you know.' She looked away from him and reminded herself why she was doing this. 'If I let you pay, it would mean that you were buying me.'

'If I pay, it means I'm spoiling you.'

'But you only want to spoil me because we had sex.'

'I want to spoil you because that is what people do in a relationship. That is normal behaviour, Chantal!' Driven to the point of explosion by the conversation, he ran his fingers through her hair. 'This conversation is going round and round in circles, and I don't even want to be talking.'

'I don't want to talk, either,' she whispered, her heart pounding as his bronzed fingers slid over her shoulder and toyed with the narrow strap of her costume. 'Take the money and the conversation ends.'

He bent his head and touched her shoulder with his mouth. 'I will *not* take the money.' His mouth was hot against her flesh and her eyes drifted shut.

'Yesterday you thought I was a gold-digger and you weren't very pleased about it. Now I'm trying to pay and you're not very pleased about that, either. That's very contradictory behaviour.'

He lifted his head and inhaled deeply, clearly at the limits of his patience. 'All right. If it makes you more comfortable, I will take the money.' He lifted the roll of cash and tucked it into his pocket with an exaggerated flourish. 'Satisfied?'

'Yes.' Her heart bumped hard against her chest. 'I'm glad you agree with me.'

'At this precise moment I'm prepared to agree to just about anything. Anything you want, the answer is yes. *Now* can we stop talking?'

She gave a tremulous smile and slid her arms round his neck. 'You understand what I'm saying?'

'No, but I'm willing to do anything you say,' he growled, his tongue probing gently as he yanked her hard against him. 'Let's go to bed. Now. Before you think up some other crazy rule.'

CHAPTER EIGHT

THREE days later, Angelos lounged in his glass-fronted office in the villa, trying to concentrate on the page of figures in front of him, his normally razor-sharp mind as blunt as a spoon.

It was only three hours since he'd left Chantal lying in bed and all he wanted to do was return there and pick up where they'd left off. It didn't matter how long he spent with her, he just wanted more. In fact his hunger had grown to the point where all he could think of was sex.

It was the first time in his life that he'd found a woman to be more absorbing than work. In fact, right at this moment, work seemed like nothing more than an irritating necessity—something to do while Chantal slept off the physical excesses of the night.

Witnessing her stunned reaction to her own sexuality had proved to be indescribably erotic. He'd discovered that there was something infinitely exciting about a passionate woman with absolutely no knowledge of the powers of her own body.

And that was the key to his current problem. She'd been a virgin, which made the whole experience a novelty, and she just adored sex, which doubled the excitement.

In the circumstances, it was hardly surprising that his mind wasn't on his work.

Staring at the complex spreadsheet on the screen in front of him, he wondered whether to abandon the pretence of working and just indulge in a two week long marathon sex session, designed to cure his obsession with her.

Why not?

He didn't believe in micro-management. He employed the very best and expected them to get on with the jobs they were being paid to do. Theoretically he should be able to take a break, if that was what he wanted.

And it was.

Given the choice, he would have been hauling her back to bed at every conceivable opportunity during the day. At coffee-time, at lunchtime, after every frustrating phone call—

But that wasn't an option because she was never around during the day.

On the few occasions he'd prowled onto the terrace, intending to surprise her, he'd discovered that she'd left after breakfast and had no intention of returning until teatime. He felt vaguely irritated by the length of time she spent away from the villa each day. For a woman who claimed not to enjoy shopping, she spent a great deal of time—well, shopping. Or was she sightseeing?

Whichever—she certainly wasn't lying by the pool dreaming of him and hoping for a midday rendezvous.

He frowned. Perhaps she thought she was doing him a favour by not distracting him from his work. Or possibly she was lonely. It was true that when his father wasn't resting he was kept busy all day with physiotherapists, nurses and doctors.

Or was she playing a more complicated game altogether?

While it was true that she was very inexperienced, it was also true that she was a woman, with a woman's instincts. Did she think that by staying out all day she would make him all the more desperate for her?

If so, then her plan was succeeding beyond her wildest dreams.

He was so desperate he was climbing the walls.

Remembering the erotic activities of the night before, Angelos decided that there was nothing going on in his working day that couldn't be put off until tomorrow. He'd join her shopping or sightseeing or whatever it was she was doing, make it clear that by staying out all day she was *not* doing him a favour and then he'd bring her back to the villa for a relaxing swim and a siesta.

Chantal delivered a large lunch order to the group of English tourists who were sitting at the best table in the taverna. 'Two moussaka, one souvlaki, one meatballs—'

It was impossibly hot, her feet ached, and she was exhausted after yet another night without sleep. She would have given anything to have spent the day sleeping by the pool.

Anything except her pride.

'Large Greek salad.' As she placed the plate in the centre of the table she heard the deep, throaty growl of a high performance sports car from somewhere behind her.

One of the men glanced towards the sound. 'That's my dream car,' he muttered enviously, reaching for his beer. 'When I have my mid-life crisis, I'm ditching my sensible family car and buying that piece of premium engineering.'

'Hummus and taramasalata—' Feeling as though she was going to melt in the heat, Chantal deposited the last of the dishes on the table. 'Can I get you anything else?'

Her question received no response. The men were listing every component of the car and the women were apparently similarly entranced.

One leaned towards the other. 'Incredible body,' she breathed, and her friend gave a feline smile.

'Devastating. Monumental sex appeal.'

It took a moment for Chantal to realise that the women were talking about the driver, not the car. The nerves on the back of her neck prickled and she turned.

Angelos slammed the car door and then strode into the res-

taurant as if he owned it, his hair glinting blue black in the glare
of the sun. His gaze cool and confident, he scanned the tables,
apparently unaware of the level of interest his arrival had created.

Then he saw her, and the flash of sexual hunger in his eyes
was immediate and unmistakable.

Chantal felt her knees weaken and the look they shared held
such intimacy that they might have been back in the bedroom.

'Obviously he's taken,' the woman behind her murmured regretfully, but Chantal barely heard her because her heart was
bumping against her chest and now she felt as though her body
was melting on the inside as well as the outside.

She gave him a faltering smile and walked over to him.

'Hello. This is a surprise. Can I get you a drink?'

'*What* do you think you're doing?' His voice was dangerously
soft and out of the corner of her eye Chantal saw the owner of
the taverna approach.

'Working. And I can't really talk to you now. It's lunchtime
and we're very busy.' She started to move away, but strong fingers
clamped around her wrist like a vice.

'You're *working*?' His voice rang with disbelief. 'What do you
mean, *working*?'

'Well—' She cleared her throat, unsure how to answer. 'I do
a job and get paid for it. It's a fairly standard formula. And I really
need to go now, because this is our busiest time and—'

'*Why?*'

'You're asking an awful lot of obvious questions.' Casting an
apologetic smile at the taverna owner, she tried once again to free
herself. 'I'm working for the same reason everyone else works.
Because I need the money.'

His eyes narrowed. 'Before this moment I never considered
myself to be stupid, but I honestly cannot think of a reason why
you would need money. I gave you my credit card.'

'I need my *own* money.'

'You are entitled to treat my credit card as your own.'

She looked at him in exasperation. 'I need proper money.'

'This is the twenty first century. A credit card *is* proper money,' he drawled, a sardonic gleam in his eyes. 'What do you need this "proper money" for?'

'All the normal things. But mostly to pay *you*. So using your credit card wouldn't have helped. I can hardly use your own money to pay you, can I? It rather defeats the object.'

There was an ominous silence. 'You are working so that you can pay me? That's where the money you gave me the other afternoon came from?' He glanced around the restaurant. 'You have been spending the last three days working here?'

'Yes.' Seeing the shock in his eyes, she felt suddenly defensive. 'What's wrong with that? Your father is busy during the day, and you're working. We don't all have a Swiss bank account full of hidden billions. I've already used up all the money I brought with me.' Aware that virtually everyone in the restaurant was following their exchange, she tried again to move away, but his grip tightened.

'We need to talk.'

'Maybe. But not now and not here.' Mortified, she glanced around her. 'Everyone is staring, Angelos.'

He frowned slightly and turned his head, taking in the gaping diners in a glance. Two streaks of colour highlighted his impressive cheekbones and he drew in a slow, deep breath. 'We need to leave this place.'

'*You* leave. I'm not going anywhere. You may not think much of this job but it's the only one I have. And if you don't let me go, so that I can serve those people over there, then I won't have it for long.'

'It doesn't matter. Because you won't be coming back here again.' Treating the customers to a full-on display of Greek volatility, Angelos fired several incomprehensible sentences in the direction of the taverna-owner, who nodded vigorously.

'My apologies.' He waved his hands towards Chantal, dismissing her hastily. 'I didn't know who you were.'

'What's that supposed to mean?' As the taverna-owner backed away and started clearing tables himself, Chantal looked at Angelos. 'Who does he think I am?'

'Mine,' Angelos said silkily, pulling her towards him with a purposeful movement that was unmistakably possessive. 'And now we are *both* leaving.' Without waiting to hear her response he walked towards the car, his firm grip on her wrist giving her no choice but to follow.

'Angelos, wait!' She took two strides to his one, jogging to keep up with him. 'This is my job.'

'Not any more. He is going to find someone else to serve his customers.'

'You can't do that! I don't want you to do that.' Chantal dug her heels in, jerked her arm and freed herself. 'I need to work.'

'Not if the purpose of working is to give me money that I don't want.' He swung her off her feet and deposited her in the passenger seat. 'We'll continue this conversation somewhere more private. I *hate* public scenes.'

'Then stop giving people something to stare at! For crying out loud, Angelos—'

'I *don't* want you working,' he growled, springing into the car with the athletic grace of a jungle cat. 'You don't need to work.'

'Yes, I do. If you won't let me pay, then I'll feel as though I'm your—'

'You're my *what*?' Simmering with anger, he trod hard on the accelerator and the car sped away from the waterfront with a throaty roar. 'What are you, Chantal? How do you see yourself?' His anger simmered like a pot of boiling oil and instead of responding she cast a desperate glance over her shoulder.

The restaurant was already fading into the distance. 'Angelos, take me back! *Please.*'

'You are *not* working in that place.'

She sighed and slumped in her seat. 'Have you any idea how hard it was to persuade him to give me that job?'

'I don't want to think about it.'

'I don't understand why you're so angry.'

'Don't you?' He changed gears viciously. 'Seeing my woman serving drinks in a bar doesn't generally do much for my mood.'

His woman?

'You sound like a caveman.' The phrase was possessive, and yet it sent a thrill through her body. No matter how much she tried to remind herself that expecting anything from this man was asking for heartbreak, she couldn't help the feeling of happiness that bathed her entire being.

'Fine. So I sound like a caveman.' His harsh tone held not one hint of regret. 'Get used to it. That's the man I am.'

'What about equality?'

'You're forgetting.' At the last minute he braked and took a sharp bend with consummate skill. 'I celebrate individuality. Men and women are different. They're supposed to be different.'

She didn't need him to point out their differences when they were right in front of her nose. Swamped by a feeling of helpless longing, it was a struggle for her to remember her principles. 'It isn't all about you, Angelos. I'm here, too.'

'It is you who I am thinking about!' His usually flawless English faltered slightly. 'Are you seriously telling me that you'd rather stand on your feet all day slogging your guts out for a minimum wage than lie by my pool being pampered?'

'Actually, yes. Because we're having an—' she stumbled over the terminology '—intimate relationship—I can't let you pay for me.'

'If we *weren't* having an intimate relationship then I wouldn't be paying for you.' Visibly exasperated, he muttered something in Greek under his breath. 'I admire your principles, but you are taking this too far. It ends now.'

'You still think I'm just doing it to impress you?' It occurred to her that they were driving away from the harbour, up into the hills, and now he was negotiating a series of terrifying hairpin bends, his eyes fixed on the road, his knuckles white as he gripped the wheel.

'Yes, but I blame myself for that. My comments on Isabelle Ducat and also on my father's ex-wives were hardly flattering. But they were *not* aimed at you. I have *never* applied those comments to you. You are different.'

'Yes, I'm different.' She clutched her seat, wishing he'd slow down. 'I don't want to be a kept woman. I need to pay my own way. I need to be useful.'

'I can think of a million ways in which you can be useful and none of them involve you balancing plates in a busy restaurant. I want no more talk about working and no more talk about paying me.'

'This isn't about you, Angelos.' Her hair blew across her face and she anchored it with her hand. 'It's about me. Even if you hadn't mentioned those other women, I still would have insisted on paying.'

'Why?'

'Because it's necessary. To not pay would make me feel like a—' She broke off, realising that she'd led the conversation up a dark, dangerous road that she didn't want to travel ever again. But it was too late.

With a smooth movement he swung the wheel and stopped the car by the side of the road in a shower of dust. Then he turned towards them, his eyes dangerously stormy. 'How would it make you feel? Tell me. I want to know.'

Her heart was thumping. 'Well—'

'*Say it!*'

'As though you're paying me to have sex.'

'You are saying that I make you feel like a prostitute?'

The word made her shrink inside. 'No! I'm not saying that—'

'Have I *ever* offered you money in exchange for sex?' His

voice was harsh and she shook her head, struggling with the feeling of nausea that threatened to overtake her.

'No, but—'

'There is no but. The answer is just *no*.' His mouth tightened. 'Do you think I brought you to Greece with the intention of seducing you?'

'No, but this is just normal behaviour for you, and you're angry because I'm not conforming. You have relationships all the time and I'm willing to bet there's a standard pattern. You sleep with a woman, you shower her with jewels until you become bored and then you move onto the next one.' *Why, oh why, had she ever started this conversation?*

'Normal behaviour?' He watched her for a moment, a tiny muscle working in his lean jaw. 'Let me remind you how "normal" my behaviour has been so far, *agape mou*. Four days ago I made love to you in my swimming pool, which just happens to be situated on the terrace in full view of most of the villa—'

Her cheeks warmed. 'You're a very sexual man.'

'I'm also a very private man,' he gritted. 'With an extraordinarily short attention span and an antisocial work habit. All those traits seem to have vanished since you arrived in Greece.'

'You've worked every day since we arrived.'

'Since we arrived I have spent approximately eighteen minutes at my computer, and most of that was spent unravelling a problem I caused by *not* concentrating.'

As the significance of his words slowly dawned on her, she wondered whether the anger in his tone was directed at himself or her. 'You're having trouble concentrating?'

He was silent for a moment, his fingers drumming an impatient rhythm on the steering wheel. '*Never* have I spent so much time achieving so little.' It was as if the confession had been dragged from him and she was silent while she tried to work out why that piece of information should make her feel light-headed.

'*I'm* the reason your concentration is affected?'

'Yes.'

'Well—' Discovering that her mouth was dry, Chantal ran her tongue over her lower lip and tried not to allow herself to read too much into it. 'I suppose that's pretty normal in a new relationship.'

'It isn't normal for me.' He spoke the words with almost violent emphasis. 'Neither is arguing in a public place, forgetting contraception, or taking the wrong road when I'm driving. None of those things constitute my normal behaviour.'

Chantal glanced over her shoulder, her heart bumping so hard she could hardly breathe. 'This is the wrong road?'

Exasperation lighting his dark eyes, he gestured impatiently to the olive groves that clung to the mountain side. 'Do you see a harbour?'

'I assumed you'd come this way on purpose.'

'I was so blind with anger to find you serving food to a lot of rude, ungrateful tourists that I turned left instead of right.' He glared at her. '*Why* is that funny?'

The darkness inside her had melted away and she couldn't stop smiling. 'Can't you see the funny side?'

'There *is* no funny side,' he said angrily. 'I hate feeling like this.'

'Out of control…' She placed a hand on his thigh, feeling the hard muscle flex beneath her fingers. 'You're not a man who likes to be out of control.'

With a driven sigh, he rubbed the tips of his fingers across his forehead. 'Jannis is probably organising a search party as we speak.' His reluctant confession was oddly endearing and Chantal felt happiness burst to life inside her.

She couldn't help it. Even though she knew it was foolish and risky to dream, the fact that she was having such an effect on him made her feel good.

'Poor Jannis… So—' her eyes were drawn to the dark hairs on his arms '—if your behaviour isn't normal, what are we going to do?'

'For a start, I'm taking you back to the villa so that I don't have to waste part of my working day tracking you down,' he growled, sliding a hand behind her head and drawing her towards him. 'From now on I want to know where you are every minute of the day. I want you where I can find you.'

His mouth was so close to hers that she could hardly breathe. 'I have to check in and out?'

'No, because you won't be going anywhere. From now on your world revolves around the bedroom and the pool.' He breathed the words against her mouth and her head swam and her eyes drifted shut.

She knew she ought to make some sort of protest, but she was desperate for him to kiss her and she didn't want to delay that activity by speaking. Instead she leaned towards him, closing the distance, unable to resist the passion that drew them together.

He kissed her with devastating expertise, his mouth hungry and demanding, but as her body was consumed by ferocious excitement she made a final, desperate attempt to protect her principles. 'I *need* to work.'

'You'll be too busy to work,' he vowed thickly, his hand stroking her ribcage and resting just short of her breast. 'You're going to forget this nonsense about working.'

The blood was pounding in her veins and she felt drugged and desperate. She just couldn't concentrate on anything when he was this close.

Resolving to find a different way to satisfy her principles, she gave up on the idea of returning to the taverna. Her body was on fire and all she wanted to do was go back to the villa. 'Do you think you can find your way back to the harbour? If you don't like public displays then I think we should go back really quickly, before we embarrass ourselves more than we already have.'

Casting a searing look in her direction, he started the engine and turned the car.

* * *

Later that evening, Angelos strolled onto the terrace for dinner,
replete and re-energized after an *extremely* satisfying afternoon.
A marathon session of explosive, steamy sex had been followed
by a profitable work session, his concentration sharpened by the
knowledge that Chantal was now safely confined to the villa.
He'd left her sated and deliciously sleepy, but already he was
looking forward to the night ahead.

She was the most responsive woman he'd ever known.

His father was already seated at the table, a glass of iced
lemonade in one hand, the newspaper in the other. 'Have you
seen the share price?'

'No.' His mind a long way from the share price, Angelos
pulled out the chair opposite and was just wondering where
Chantal was when she appeared in the doorway that led from the
kitchen.

She was balancing several dishes, the tip of her tongue caught
between her teeth as she tried not to drop them.

Remembering the last time he'd seen her cheeks that flushed,
Angelos gave a lazy smile and sat back in his chair. 'Why are
you serving food? Has Maria had an accident?'

'No, she's busy talking to the dietician.' Carefully she placed
a dish of grilled fish and lemon slices in front of Costas, and then
put a dish in front of Angelos. 'Try it,' she urged, her eyes spark-
ling with pride. 'I want to know what you think.'

Captivated by the triumph in her expression, it took Angelos
a moment to drag his eyes from her face to the food in front of
him. 'You want my opinion on moussaka?'

'On this moussaka, yes. Because I made it. And I did something special with the aubergines.' Breathless with anticipation,
she watched his face anxiously. 'Does it look all right? Maria said
it was good, but I think she was just being kind.'

Unable to hide his astonishment, Angelos stared at her. 'You
cooked? When?' Noticing the satisfied smile on his father's face,

he realised just how much his question had revealed about their afternoon activity.

'Maria taught me. We made *dolmades*, too. Pretty fiddly, but I did OK, I think.' Beaming with pride, Chantal slid into the seat next to him and waited expectantly. 'Are you going to try it?'

Angelos was still adjusting to the fact that she'd surprised him yet again.

She hadn't been lying in bed, recovering. She'd been slaving in the kitchen, in the heat, cooking him dinner. 'Why?'

'Because you need to eat.'

'No.' His tone was impatient as he searched for an answer to his question. 'I mean why are you cooking for me when I employ Maria for that task? You should have been relaxing.'

'Maria is very busy shopping and preparing your father's special diet, and she has the whole of the villa to look after. If I can cook, then I can help her.'

'You don't need to help her.' His words drew her gaze, and suddenly there was a stubborn tilt to her chin that he hadn't seen before.

'You won't let me earn money, so this will be my contribution.'

'I don't *want* your contribution.' He saw the hurt in her eyes and cursed himself for being tactless. 'I don't mean that I don't want the food. I just mean that you don't need to cook.'

'Yes, I do.' She reached forward and served herself a generous helping. 'You're very old-fashioned—do you know that?'

Angelos drew a deep breath. 'I am certainly *not* old-fashioned.'

'You are. You don't want a woman to work. You're not comfortable with the whole concept of equality.' She dissected the food on her plate with a fork, examining each layer with the delight of a child opening a present. 'You think a woman should spend her life on a sun lounger, ready for you whenever you want to take a break from your pressing work schedule.'

'That is *not* true.'

'Then why did you make me give up my job?'

Costas looked interested. 'Job? What job?'

'I found myself a job in a taverna.' Chantal smiled at his father. 'But Angelos didn't want me working there.'

Costas chuckled. 'I'm starting to understand why he has been so bad-tempered during the day.'

'I have *not* been bad-tempered.' Angelos lifted his wine. 'And it is ridiculous to suggest that I don't want women to work. A large proportion of my senior executives are women.'

'But I'm ready to bet that they're not women you have relationships with,' Chantal said mildly. 'I'm sure you neatly separate your work and social life. Which makes you hypocritical as well as old-fashioned. You're happy for a woman to work, just not *your* woman. From that I assume you usually date heiresses.'

It occurred to him that he'd never felt so out of control of a conversation. 'Why would you assume that?'

'Because you don't want women to take your money, but you don't want them to make their own money, either. That rules out a large chunk of the population and really only leaves heiresses.'

Aware that his father was following the exchange with delight, Angelos gritted his teeth. 'This conversation is pointless.'

'You're just saying that because you're losing the argument.' She looked at his plate. 'Aren't you at least going to try the moussaka? I think it's very good. I'm proud of it.'

'Most women would be delighted that a man is prepared to support them,' Angelos growled as he picked up his fork. 'Just because I don't happen to think a woman should pay when she's in a relationship with me, it doesn't make me old-fashioned or hypocritical.'

'But you're very wary that a woman might only be interested in your money. Which makes it all rather contradictory, doesn't it? It makes the whole thing very confusing for you, and even more confusing for me.'

Costas started to laugh, and once he started he couldn't stop, the spasms shaking his body. 'That has to be the first time a woman has ever beaten you in an argument. Come to think of it, she's probably the first woman you've ever spent time with who can string a sentence together. She's perfect, Angelos.' He reached for a napkin and mopped his eyes, trying to get himself under control. 'An original, just like your mother. That woman always tied me in knots. Manipulated me into saying all sorts of things I didn't mean.'

'Was she an heiress?' Chantal asked the question with interest, and Angelos watched as his father's gaze misted again.

'She was just a girl,' Costas said gruffly. 'A girl that I loved. And I would have loved her the same way whether she'd been rich or poor. And she could cook. That is where I went wrong with the other two. They couldn't cook.'

'Why would they need to? They didn't eat,' Angelos pointed out dryly, and his father shuddered.

'Do *not* remind me.' He looked longingly across the table. 'Perhaps I should try the moussaka?'

'The doctor wanted you to eat the fish,' Chantal said firmly, 'and it's delicious. Maria and I baked it in lemon and Greek herbs. Try it. I want to know if you like it. If not, I'll strike it off our list. We're trying something different every day.' She watched expectantly, a sparkle in her eyes, and Costas obediently picked up his fork and ate.

'So you went and found yourself a job?'

'That's right.' She heaped his plate with salad. 'Obviously there's limited opportunity for employment around here, but I needed the money.'

Costas sampled the fish. 'It's delicious.'

'You like it? Really?' Delighted, Chantal smiled, and Angelos found himself staring hungrily at her mouth. It didn't matter whether she was smiling, talking or kissing—her mouth was incredible.

Costas was devouring his food with enthusiasm. 'Don't listen to Angelos. You can cook for me again tomorrow. If it tastes like this, you can cook for me every day.'

'I'll bring the menus to you and you can tell me what you like best. We can adapt them together.' Chantal reached across the table and took the salt from his hand. '*Don't* add salt,' she scolded gently. 'It isn't good for you.'

'I like salt.'

'The herbs should give you all the seasoning you need.'

Angelos lounged in his chair, watching the spirited interchange in amused silence. It had been years since he'd seen his father so relaxed and content.

Not since his mother was alive.

And there was no doubt who was responsible for the change in him.

Chantal.

She sampled the food on her own plate tentatively, chewing slowly. Then she gave a low, appreciative murmur, the sound so sensual and evocative that his body hardened in an instantaneous response.

Watching her across the table, he decided that his father was correct about one thing—there was something indescribably erotic about a woman who enjoyed her food.

She glanced at him and paused with the fork halfway to her mouth. 'You're not eating. Is something wrong?'

Angelos glanced at his plate and realised that he'd forgotten to eat. 'It's too hot.'

'No, it's not. Maria told me you prefer it served slightly cooler, so that's what I did. Don't you like it?'

'It's delicious.'

'Then what's the matter?' She put her fork down, her gaze self conscious. 'You're staring at me.'

She was the matter. She had a volcanic effect on his libido.

Suddenly he couldn't wait for the meal to end so that he could take her back to bed.

'He is not used to being with a woman who eats,' Costas said cheerfully. 'The sight is as rare as a snow leopard in the middle of Athens.'

Aware that the faster he ate, the sooner the evening would end, Angelos swiftly finished the food on his plate and then served himself an extra helping just to please her.

He ate quickly, but was forced to wait until his father and Chantal had finished discussing the relative merits of different forms of exercise.

Finally his father yawned and excused himself. Immediately Angelos rose and led Chantal back into the bedroom.

'Don't you want coffee?' She gave a gasp as he pulled her hard against him.

'No,' he growled, his mouth sliding down the inviting curve of her neck. 'I don't want coffee. Nor do I want fruit or conversation. In fact, *agape mou*, the only thing I want is you. Naked. Right now.'

Her head tilted back and her eyes drifted shut. 'Don't do that. I can't think when you do that—'

'I don't want you to think.'

'Angelos…' She gave a low whimper. 'We only got out of bed a few hours ago.'

'*That* was a mistake. We should never have left the bed.' He stroked a hand over the curve of her bottom and it was his turn to groan. 'I can't decide whether this is your best feature. I need you naked so that I can assess all your qualities together.'

Her fingers dug into his shoulder. 'My bottom is too big.'

'Your bottom is perfect. *You* are perfect. Even my father adores you,' he said as he bent his head and kissed her neck. 'You are playing an important part in his recovery and I'm grateful for that. Don't think I don't know that you are the reason he's eating properly, and has swapped his wine for juice and water.'

'I adore him.' She pulled away slightly and gave a faltering smile. 'In fact, I envy you.'

'You do?' His eyes narrowed. It was the first time she'd shown any interest in his financial status.

'Yes, you're incredibly lucky. I'd do anything to have a father like yours.'

It wasn't the comment he'd been expecting, and it took a moment for her words to register. 'You envy me my *father*?'

'Yes.' She looked into his eyes and then frowned slightly. 'Why? What did you think I was going to say?'

Deciding that this was one of those occasions when it was best not to be honest, Angelos stayed silent, but she breathed in sharply and stepped away from him. 'You assumed I envied you your wealth.' She watched him for a moment and then gave a little laugh. 'You still don't know me at all, do you?'

'It was a natural assumption. No one has envied me my father before.'

'I'm sure they have. He's lovely.' There was something in her wistful tone that caught his attention.

'Is your own father alive?'

He saw her sudden tension, and then she pulled away from him. 'He and my mother didn't—' She stopped. 'They didn't stay in touch. I have no idea where he is now.'

'You've never tried to trace him?'

She stilled, her back to him. 'No.'

'Is he the source of your insecurities?' Angelos put his hands on her shoulders and turned her to face him. 'Is he the reason you have a low opinion of yourself?'

For a moment she didn't answer, and then she raised herself on tiptoe and brushed her mouth against his. 'Just kiss me, Angelos,' she murmured huskily. 'Stop talking and kiss me.'

He realised just how little he knew about her life, but the blood was pounding in his head and the touch of her mouth against his drove all rational thought from his head. Since when had it become a challenge to concentrate on anything?

All he wanted to do was rip her clothes off and explore her lush, spectacular body in minute detail.

Driven by the thunderous force of his libido, Angelos tumbled her back onto the bed and brought his mouth down on hers, his hands swiftly removing her clothes from her deliciously squirming body.

'*Angelos*, please—' Her soft whimper of desperation removed every last scrap of his self-control and the need to satisfy his sexual hunger took precedence over everything else.

With something close to desperation he came down on top of her and immediately she parted her legs, her silky-soft thighs brushing against his as she arched expectantly.

Responding to an urge so powerful that it went far beyond anything he had experienced before, he thrust into her soft, damp core, her immediate moan of pleasure adding still more fuel to his passion. She was hot and tight and he was so overwhelmed by how good she felt that he drove deep in his need to satisfy the almost agonising attack of lust that gripped him.

Her nails dug into his shoulders and she gasped his name one more time and then he felt the orgasm ripple through her body, drawing him over the edge.

His world exploded and he thrust hard, swallowing her whimpers of ecstasy with the demands of his mouth as he emptied his body into hers.

In the aftermath, neither of them spoke. *Neither of them was able to speak*.

After what seemed like an age, Angelos rolled back against the pillows and gathered her against him, unwilling to let her go even for a moment. 'Tell me why you were working as a cleaner.'

She didn't answer immediately. 'It was the only job I could find when I arrived in Paris.'

'Where were you before Paris?'

'Buenos Aires. I worked with horses for a while.'

'Presumably that's where you learned to tango?' He suddenly discovered that he wanted to know everything about her. He wasn't comfortable with the knowledge that he knew so little of her life. 'And before that?'

'I travelled in Peru. And before that I was in India, Australia and New Zealand…'

Listening to the endless list of countries that she'd visited, he found himself more and more intrigued. 'Obviously you're not one for putting down roots.' He rolled onto his side so that he could look at her, but immediately her eyes slid from his.

'I'm not really a roots sort of person. I just wanted to travel.'

'Did you go to university?' Even though he was looking at her profile he saw something alter in her expression.

'No.' Her tone was flat. 'I didn't.'

'But you're obviously very bright—'

'I didn't do that well at school. I didn't like school. Can we talk about something else?' She sat up sharply, as if something had upset her. 'What about you? Tell me how you came to make your billions.'

Judging from her tense expression that it was best to allow her the change of subject, Angelos tugged her back down into his arms. 'I didn't like school, either. I found it very restricting. I wanted to do things my way.'

The tension in her body eased and she relaxed against him. 'I expect you had to be first in everything?'

'Of course.'

A bubble of laughter escaped her lips. 'You haven't changed much, have you?'

'No.' Pleased to see her back to her good natured self, Angelos continued to talk. 'My father was a very successful man. He wanted me to join his business.'

'But you didn't.'

'Of course not. Where would be the challenge in that? I had

no desire to be a caretaker for a business that someone else had developed.'

'So you did your own thing.' She slid her arm around him. 'It's nice to know that you're vulnerable, like everyone else.'

Vulnerable?

Startled by her interpretation of his motives, Angelos frowned up at the ceiling. '*How* am I vulnerable?'

'You obviously wanted to prove something to your father.'

Considering that possibility for the first time in his life, Angelos gave a surprised laugh. 'You're probably right—but don't tell my competitors. If they hear a rumour that I'm vulnerable, my working life will become far more challenging and I will have less time to spend in bed with you.'

'I expect your father is very proud of you.' There was a wistful note in her voice that caught his attention.

'What about you?' Deciding that he'd backed off enough, he gently eased the subject back to her own childhood. 'If your father wasn't around, then presumably it was your mother who brought you up? Where did you live?'

'We moved around a lot when I was young, and then later I was at boarding school. That's enough talking for now. I'm tired, Angelos. Goodnight.' She rolled over so that her back was facing him and tugged the silk sheet up over her shoulders, the gesture clearly declaring that the subject was closed.

Angelos stared in silence at her tense body, his mind working overtime.

It was obvious that she found any mention of her mother, her childhood or her schooldays extraordinarily stressful. Obviously it hadn't been a good time for her, and yet it was equally obvious that she was bright and intelligent and should have excelled.

He wanted to continue the conversation—*he wanted to understand her*—and that thought troubled him, because he'd never before had the slightest inclination to understand a woman.

Deciding that he would achieve more by continuing the conversation when she was more relaxed, he lay down and pulled her into his arms.

He didn't mind her sleeping with her back to him, but there was no way he was allowing her to shut herself off.

CHAPTER NINE

'PACK a bag,' Angelos instructed as he emerged from the shower with droplets of water still clinging to his bronzed skin. A towel was looped casually around his hips, leaving his torso bare.

He would have made a Greek god sob with envy, Chantal thought as she stared at the smooth, well-defined muscles of his shoulders. Secretly she was hoping that he might decide to come back to bed.

'Why do I need to pack a bag? I don't want to leave here.' She knew she sounded desperate, but she couldn't help it.

She'd been so incredibly happy. Happier than she'd ever been in her life before.

And she didn't want it to end.

She still couldn't believe that two weeks had passed already.

'We're not leaving.' Reaching for his watch, he cast her an amused glance. 'I'm glad you like it here.'

'I love it.' She loved *him*. It didn't matter how many times she reminded herself that this relationship wasn't going anywhere, she still couldn't control her feelings.

She loved him, she loved his father, and she loved the island. They were protected from the outside world and at times it felt as though real life would never intrude again.

He raked strands of damp hair out of his eyes. 'Then you will be pleased to hear that we're not leaving yet. But we have to go to Athens for two days.'

'Athens?' Dragging her eyes from the tantalising line of hair that disappeared below the towel, Chantal sat up, the sheet clutched to her chest. 'Why?'

'Unfortunately my lengthy absence from work has created a few problems which require my personal attention.' Without elaborating, he vanished into the dressing room and emerged with a crisp white shirt in his hand.

'You go,' she said quickly. 'I'll stay here.'

'No way. I've already learned that I can't concentrate on my work unless you are around. Where I go, you go. That's the deal.' He released the towel and she had a brief glimpse of his magnificent torso before he slipped his arms into the shirt. Her stomach plummeted and she wished for the millionth time that she wasn't so receptive to him. It was as if her body had been created to respond to his.

'I don't want to go to Athens.' Swamped by a feeling of fore-boding, she wrapped her arms around her knees and searched for plausible excuses. 'We can't leave your father on his own.'

'He has a doctor, two nurses and a dietician.' Angelos finished dressing swiftly. 'Not to mention Maria. And it is just for one night. I'll spend this afternoon in the office, then we will attend the function, stay the night in my house in Athens, and then return.'

'Function?'

He reached for a tie. 'Another fundraising occasion. Unfortunately my presence is mandatory.'

Wondering if she would ever become indifferent to his body, Chantal watched as he fastened the button at his bronzed throat. 'If you're spending the evening at a function, then I might as well wait for you here. It's not as if I'll get to spend time with you.'

'I'm not leaving you here.'

'I don't want to go.' Defensive as a child, she watched him

warily. 'I'll be totally out of place at something like that. You know I will.'

'Why would you be out of place?'

'Because I'm not like the people in your world.'

'This is my world,' he said smoothly, prowling over to the bed and bending down to kiss her once again, 'and you are in it.'

But she was only in it because he was enjoying the sex. There was nothing more to it than that. *Not even at her most deluded had she ever pretended she was part of his world.* 'Being here is different from going out to that sort of event. I don't fit.'

He stroked her hair away from her face. 'You went to the ball in Paris.'

'And that was a mistake.'

'A mistake, *agape mou*?' He gave a slow, sexy smile. 'I don't think so.'

'All right—meeting you wasn't a mistake. But the ball itself was a mistake. I felt totally out of place. And this time I won't have your father to save me.'

'*Save* you?' His dark brows met in a sudden frown. 'Who will you need saving from?'

She looked away from him, feeling the darkness closing in. *He had no idea what her life had been like.* 'It just isn't me, Angelos. Forget it.'

'*Don't* look away from me.' He slid a hand over her cheek and turned her head towards him. 'And don't try and hide what you're thinking. I want to know everything about you.'

But she didn't *want* him to know everything. He already knew far more than most people.

She forced herself to smile. 'Then you should know that I feel out of place at glittering functions. You go to Athens. But come back quickly.'

'I can't believe you don't want to go.' A trace of exasperation in his expression, he studied her face. 'You are the only woman

've ever met who isn't always looking for an excuse to dress up
nd party.'

'If that's what you want, then go and find a woman who
njoys parties.'

'I'm with the woman I want to be with. You have no reason
ɔ feel insecure.'

'I'm not insecure,' she lied, and then blushed as he lifted an
yebrow in silent challenge. 'Oh, all right—maybe I am a little
nsecure. But only in certain situations.'

'You have no reason to be insecure in *any* situation.'

'I just feel—' she hesitated '—different.'

'You *are* different.' He rose to his feet with his usual athletic
grace. 'Which is why I am with you. You are generous, and
eautiful, and you care about the things that matter.'

'*I don't fit*.' She tried to reason with him. 'At that ball in Paris,
veryone was staring at me.'

'Because you are beautiful,' he said dryly. 'You were more
eautiful than any other woman in the room that night in Paris.
And a million times more genuine. You have no reason to have
uch a low opinion of yourself.'

'It's just that I'm not comfortable going to events like that.'

'How many have you attended?'

Chantal coloured. 'Just the one.'

'And you were gatecrashing, rather than arriving as an invited
guest,' he drawled softly, 'so it was hardly surprising that you
vere on tenterhooks for the whole evening. Come with me
onight. You will have fun.'

'I won't know anyone—'

'You will know me.' Supremely confident that his presence
vould be more than enough for anyone, he strolled across the
oom and picked up his jacket. 'Don't argue with me.'

He just didn't understand.

She tried a different approach. 'I don't have anything suitable
ɔ wear.'

'Now you are talking like a woman.' He smiled. 'We will find you something to wear that will give you confidence.'

But she knew only too well that confidence came from the inside, not the outside. And what was inside her was so foul that it tarnished the baby shoots of her confidence like some malevolent pest. 'I don't want to go, Angelos.'

'Pack,' he ordered, his tone firm. 'You have nothing to worry about. I will be there with you. If you need saving, then I will save you.'

But he didn't understand what threatened her, did he?

What did he know about insecurity or lack of confidence? He was super-bright, highly educated and immensely successful. And his home-life had clearly been both loving and supportive.

She stared at him helplessly, swamped by a feeling of foreboding that couldn't be ignored.

It didn't matter how firmly she told herself that she was wrong, she just knew that the idyll was over.

Their fabulous two weeks was about to end with a bang.

This was the other side of his life, Chantal thought as the private helicopter swooped over the Greek mainland towards Athens. Closeted on his secluded island, she'd barely thought of his billionaire status. They'd been a man and a woman, nothing more. 'I didn't know the island had a helipad.'

'I rarely use it. When I go to the island, I go to relax and unwind.' Dressed in a light grey suit that emphasised his sleek dark looks, Angelos looked every inch the successful business tycoon, and his phone just didn't stop ringing.

Watching him snap into work mode to answer yet another call, Chantal studied his profile as he talked. *Why was she suddenly finding him intimidating?*

Was it the fact that he was dressed more formally than he'd been at the villa?

Reminding herself that he was the same man she'd woken up

next to that morning, she took a deep breath and tried to calm herself. But she couldn't subdue the feeling of unease that dulled the edge of the happiness she'd discovered over the past two weeks.

Angelos finished his call and glanced at her. 'As I have said I have to spend a few hours in the office this afternoon. But first I will take you shopping for something to wear this evening.'

Chantal thought about the small amount of money in her bag. 'Just don't take me anywhere ridiculously pricey.'

'I will enjoy spoiling you.'

'I don't want your money.'

'I'm not offering you money,' he drawled, leaning across and releasing the catch on her seat belt. 'I'm buying you a gift. Now stop talking about it. We've arrived.'

A plush, air-conditioned car whisked them from the airport into the centre of Athens and as they weaved through the heavy traffic, Chantal found herself intrigued by the busy, bustling city.

It was nice to see places in comfort and style, she conceded as she watched people wilting in the heat outside.

To her right she noticed a colourful market and craned her neck to get a closer look, wishing that they had time to stop and explore.

But Angelos clearly had something different in mind, and a few minutes later the driver turned into a wide road and stopped outside a glass-fronted designer boutique.

Angelos switched off his phone and urged her out onto the pavement.

The clothes in the window were frighteningly elegant and chic, but one dress in particular caught her eye. She studied it for a moment, automatically noting the cut and style and deciding how she'd adapt it if she were making it.

Angelos urged her into the shop and immediately a gaggle of sales staff converged on them, drawn by his unmistakable air of authority. He had 'billionaire' written all over him, and she could see them glancing at her simple dress and wondering what a man like him was doing with a girl like her.

Having sex, she thought gloomily. *That's what he's doing.*

Ignoring them, he glanced impatiently at his watch and turned towards her. 'Choose something.'

Just like that.

He was a man who didn't know how it felt to be intimidated by one's surroundings.

She glanced around at all the chrome and glass, wondering if she was supposed to wash her hands before she touched any of the clothes.

Ignoring the hovering sales assistants, because she knew that if she looked at them they'd destroy her fragile confidence, Chantal walked tentatively towards the dress that she'd seen in the window.

The design was ridiculously simple. It was the quality of the fabric that turned it into something special.

'It would look wonderful on you. It's cut to conceal that extra bit of weight,' an assistant murmured, and Angelos frowned.

'Then it won't suit her,' he said smoothly, 'because she doesn't have any extra weight.'

Ridiculously grateful that he'd countered the bitchy comment, Chantal stared at the dress. It was cut on the bias and she could see that it would hang well on a woman with curves.

'How much is it?'

Her question was met by appalled silence, and the assistants glanced at each other and then at Angelos, who responded with a cool stare.

'You're running a business. Surely you know the answer to that question?'

After a brief hesitation, one of the assistants cleared her throat. 'It's—' She breathed in, as though she'd never been asked that question before '—forty thousand euros.'

Chantal stepped away from the dress, feeling suddenly faint. 'That's outrageous.'

'Is it?' Angelos frowned. 'If you like it, at least try it.'

She turned towards him, her jaw set at a stubborn angle. 'At *forty thousand euros*? I don't think so.'

'The price isn't relevant.'

'Of course it's relevant. I can't afford it.'

'But I can.'

His casual statement merely reminded her of the enormous gulf between their circumstances and she shook her head, taking another step back from the dress.

'No.' Aware that the assistant was gaping at her as if she'd lost her mind, Chantal backed towards the door. 'Can we talk for a moment?'

Anglos let out an exasperated sigh and followed her out into the stifling heat of the street. 'What is going on? Stop dithering. You need something to wear this evening. You have to buy a dress. That one will do fine.'

'Why did you bring me here?' Feeling raw inside, she wrapped her arms around her body. 'Were you trying to make me look stupid or something?'

His dark eyes were suddenly wary, as if he sensed a trap. 'I brought you here to buy you a dress.'

'But that dress is *forty thousand euros*.' She almost choked on the words. 'I can't afford that.'

'Obviously I was *not* intending *you* to pay.'

Her breathing grew more rapid. 'Haven't you learned a single thing about me in the time we've been together? *I don't want your money*.'

'I wasn't offering you money,' he replied, his tone suddenly guarded. 'I was buying you a dress. A gift.'

He just didn't get it.

'I don't want a forty-thousand-euro gift. What does that say about our relationship?'

'That I care about you enough to be generous?'

'I don't want that sort of generosity. *That isn't how I want our relationship to be.*' Discovering that her eyes were swimming with tears, she blinked rapidly. 'Anyway, anyone who spends that much on a dress that someone else could be wearing too has got to be stupid.'

He drew in a long breath. 'You are very difficult to please.'

'No, I'm not. I'm easy to please. When you peel my orange for breakfast, you please me. When you rub my shoulders before I go to sleep, that pleases me. When you defend me from a nasty comment, that pleases me. *I'm easy to please, Angelos.*' Her heart was pounding. 'Just don't try and buy me.'

'I am *not* trying to buy you.' This time his tone was exasperated. 'I'm trying to spoil you. And I did not bring you here to make you look stupid. I brought you here because this is the place where every other woman of my acquaintance begs to be brought. I understood it to be retail Nirvana.'

'Not for me.'

'Obviously not. You are very complicated. Keeping pace with you requires a degree in psychology. So—' he gestured towards the row of expensive shops '—if this isn't the place for you, where do you want to go?'

'Somewhere I can afford.' On impulse she grabbed his hand and dragged him down the street towards the market they'd passed in the car.

'Where are we going?'

'To find a dress.'

'There are no boutiques in this direction. And it's forty degrees in the shade,' Angelos muttered as he strode along next to her. 'No one walks at this time of day in Athens.'

'Billionaires don't walk, but normal people *do* walk, Angelos. Just for five minutes, try living like a normal person.' She crossed the road, dodging between the frantic traffic, and found the market. 'I want to look here.'

Angelos scanned the crowded market in speechless amazement, and then jerked her against him. 'You are going to a ball. The cream of Athens society will be there. And you want to wear a dress that you have purchased from the stall of a market trader?'

'Not a dress, no—' Ignoring him, she tugged herself free from his grip and walked up and down the rows of stalls until she found what she wanted. A stall selling brightly coloured hand-printed silk. She stopped, her eyes scanning the rolls until something caught her eye. It was a deep sea-green, flecked with bright blue. 'That one, please.' Reaching into her bag, she pulled out a notebook and pencil and drew a quick sketch. Then she did some fast calculations.

'You are buying fabric?' Angelos glanced at his watch, not even bothering to conceal his irritation. 'Even with all the money at my disposal, I will not be able to find someone in Athens who will be able to make a dress for you at this late stage.'

'I'm making it myself.' Using the figures in her notebook, she ordered the fabric she needed and was delighted to find that she had enough money for the purchase.

Angelos muttered something in Greek and then switched to English. 'I was happy to buy you that dress in the shop.'

'But I wouldn't have been happy to wear it. Not unless I'd paid for it myself. Relax, Angelos. I'm happy.' She handed the money over to the man with a smile, and tucked the fabric into her bag. Then she moved onto the next stall and bought some thread, and to another, where she bought a plain hairslide and a selection of tiny shells.

Angelos watched in disbelief. 'I don't have a sewing machine in my house.'

'I sew by hand.' She made her last purchase. A tube of glue. 'I just need a couple of hours to myself, that's all. You won't miss me. You'll be on the phone. You always are.' She smiled at him. 'I don't know why you're so cross. I've saved you a fortune. And I'm happy because I paid for it myself.'

'You're *ridiculously* independent,' he breathed. 'I *wanted* to spoil you.'

Her insides melted and she stood on tiptoe to kiss him. 'Spoil me in other ways,' she said softly. 'I like being with you. It's enough.'

He stared down at her and the look in his eyes was blatantly sexual. 'Let's go home.'

Angelos glanced at his watch. If they didn't hurry up they'd be late. Not that he minded for himself. In fact, arriving late would have been his preference, but he was worried about Chantal. She was already nervous enough. He didn't want her to make a late entrance, especially when she was wearing a dress that she'd made herself from a scrap of fabric she'd bought in a market.

Didn't she realise that she was going to be exposing herself to the sort of scrutiny that she hated?

Cursing fluently, he ran a hand over the back of his neck and wished he'd just purchased the other dress and demolished her objections.

'Angelos?'

Hearing her voice, he turned. And caught his breath.

The unexceptional piece of fabric from the market had been transformed into an elegant dress. It fell from two shoestring straps, skimmed the feminine curves of her body and pooled on the floor, the hemline shimmering with tiny shells. Her sleek hair spilled like warm sunshine over her bare shoulders and a delicate bracelet of shells encircled one slender wrist. In one hand she carried a matching fabric evening bag.

She looked spectacular. And impossibly sexy. Like a mermaid allowed one night of earthly pleasure.

Lust slammed through his body with predictable force and his mouth dried.

Clearly apprehensive, she took a few steps towards him and then hesitated. 'Say something—' Her tone was light, but her expression was anxious as she watched his reaction. 'And make sure it's something nice.'

Driven by the demands of his libido, Angelos strode across to her and pulled her into his arms, anchoring her against the almost painful throb of his erection. Then he bent his head and captured her glossy mouth with his, kissing her until he felt the hard tips of her breasts press through the thin cotton of his shirt.

She sank against him for a few seconds and then dragged her mouth from his. 'You just removed *all* my lipstick,' she protested breathlessly, and Angelos wondered whether it would be risky to admit that her lipstick wasn't the only thing he wanted to remove at that moment.

'You look amazing.'

Her face brightened. 'Really? I'm not going to embarrass you?'

'No, but I might well embarrass myself if you go out looking like that.' He ran a hand over her bare shoulder. 'You look like a very, very sexy mermaid. I can't look at you without wanting to take you to bed. I can't believe you made that dress. How did you learn to sew?'

'I taught myself. You like it?' She sounded delighted, and he realised with a stab of surprise just how much he wanted her to be happy.

She still hadn't said much about her childhood, but he sensed that she'd had an *extremely* hard life and he hated the fact that she had so little confidence.

Vowing to change all that, he admired the shells on the dress. He'd never been remotely interested in women's fashions, but even he could see that what she'd produced was nothing short of spectacular.

'You should be really proud of yourself.'

Her amazing blue eyes widened. 'Should I?'

'You have an incredible talent.'

She frowned slightly, as if it hadn't occurred to her, and he felt a flash of frustration that her astonishing ability had clearly gone unrecognised for so long.

Never one to allow raw talent to go to waste, Angelos promised himself that he was going to change that.

Perhaps, if she spent enough time with him, some of his confidence would rub off on her. 'I hate to say this—' he slid his hand over the tempting curve of her bottom '—but we need to leave.'

Her smile faltered. 'We could just stay in—'

'I want to show you off.' And it was true. Not only was she stunningly beautiful, she was also bright, funny and incredibly warm-natured. 'And you have no reason to be under-confident. You will outshine every woman in the room. And they will all want to know where you bought your dress, so you'd better have some answers ready.'

The dinner was an elegant affair, attended by the cream of Athens society. They welcomed her graciously, but Chantal couldn't help but be aware of the curiosity in their eyes as they watched her and wondered.

'They're staring,' she murmured to Angelos as he placed a tall flute of champagne in her hand.

'Of course they're staring. Your dress is every bit as amazing as the one you wore in Paris.'

'I wish I'd worn something different.' Hideously self-conscious, she felt as though she were standing naked. 'They're gossiping and wondering.'

'Are they?' He slid an arm round her waist and drew her against him. 'Then we'd better give them something decent to gossip about.' He lowered his mouth to hers and kissed her gently, undoubtedly aware that the affectionate gesture was unlikely to have been missed by a single person in the room. Leisurely and unhurried, he finally lifted his head and she gave a soft gasp of disbelief.

'I thought you weren't into public displays.'

'I'm not,' he drawled, angling his head and eyeing those around him with cool disdain. 'Which just goes to prove how much you've changed me. If people wish to gossip, *agape mou*, then let them gossip. It doesn't affect us. And now I'm going to introduce you to some people who matter to me.'

His arm possessive as it rested on her waist, he drew her into the sophisticated crowd and immediately people surged forward.

He moved among them, speaking briefly to some, at greater length to others, always with authority and a natural air of command. People pressed in on them, all desperate to be associated with him in some way.

'Why does everyone want to talk to you?' Chantal touched his arm. 'Are you a genius or is it just because you're rich?'

He threw back his head and laughed and several people glanced towards them in astonishment, clearly wondering who or what had amused him so much. 'Both.' His eyes teased her gently. 'I'm a genius, and that's why I'm rich. The two invariably go together.'

'And you're arrogant. Don't forget that bit.' Laughing at him, she glanced around her. 'I just can't believe these people are all genuine.'

'They're not.' He took her hand and led her onto the terrace. Beneath them lay the city, glittering like jewelled cloth. 'I'm glad you came tonight.'

'You didn't give me any choice.' She placed a hand on his chest, keeping him slightly at a distance. *It was the only way she could concentrate.* 'We have things we need to talk about, Angelos…'

'Yes.' His voice soft, he moved slightly so that his powerful shoulders shielded her from curious guests. 'So, let's talk.'

'Here?' Surprised, she tilted her head back to look at him. 'You don't want to wait until we're home?'

'When we're home, we won't be talking.' His powerful thigh brushed suggestively against hers and she gave a stifled gasp.

'Oh—' Invisible sensuous threads were pulling them together in the semi-darkness.

'What do you want to say, Chantal?'

She could tell from his voice that he was as tightly wound as she was and she took a deep breath, trying to subdue the throbbing passion that threatened to consume both of them. 'It's time to tell your father the truth.' *He seems so much better now.*

'I agree. We'll do it tomorrow.'

'I don't want him hurt.'

'He won't be hurt. He'll be thrilled.'

'Thrilled that you lied to him?'

'When have I lied to him?' His tone was smooth and he lifted a hand and stroked a strand of hair away from her eyes. 'He believed that we were together.'

'But—'

'And we are together.'

What exactly did he mean by that? Confused, it took her a moment to speak. 'What are you saying?'

'That it doesn't end here. Did you really think I'd let you go?' He was so close now that she could feel the heat from his body, and desire curled low in her pelvis.

Her heartbeat was suddenly uneven. 'What are you suggesting?'

'Isn't it obvious? When we leave the island, you will come with me.'

His words were so unexpected that her heart stopped altogether. 'Where to?'

'Wherever I go.' Supremely confident of her response, he looked at her expectantly and her breath caught.

Why not?

He wanted her. And she wanted him. For a moment excitement flared inside her, but it was almost immediately doused. She couldn't accept, could she? *How could she possibly accept?* 'Would I be able to work?'

Astonishment shimmered in his eyes. 'Why would you want to?'

'I've already made that clear.'

'I travel a great deal. Naturally you would travel with me. So the answer is no, you would not be able to work.'

She stilled, a feeling of numbness growing inside her. 'So I'd be your kept woman?'

His eyes narrowed. 'You would be my lover. My companion. You can chose the title yourself.'

'I can't afford to be with you,' she said simply. 'Your lifestyle is too expensive. It's all private jets and fast cars and top restaurants. What I earn in a week wouldn't even cover your phone bill.'

'I am not expecting you to pay for anything. I don't *want* you to pay for anything. I will provide everything you need.'

'So what will that make me? A prostitute with one employer?'

A stunned silence followed her outburst and then he grabbed her wrist in a vice-like grip and propelled her across the balcony, through the crowded ballroom and out again into the street.

As usual everyone seemed to anticipate his wishes before he'd even expressed himself, and moments later his car purred to a halt in front of them.

For a moment Angelos just stood there, and Chantal glanced at his rigid profile.

He was angry. *So angry*. Every inch of his powerful frame vibrated with emotion and she sighed.

'Angelos— '

'Get in,' he ground out finally. 'Get in or so help me I'll put you in the car myself—and then you'll know the meaning of gossip.'

She glanced over her shoulder and realised that their rapid exit had drawn attention.

'We really—'

'Don't say another word.' He sprang into the car and flattened the accelerator to the floor, driving like an Athenian born and bred.

Anyone who thought driving in Paris was a nightmare should try Athens, Chantal though faintly, choosing to close her eyes rather than watch as Angelos zigzagged the car through the heavy traffic.

Finally he pulled in, ignoring the cars that zoomed past them at an alarming rate. 'Where are we?'

'Somewhere anonymous.' He turned to face her, his expression grim.

'I don't know why you're so angry.'

'You accuse me of treating you like a prostitute and *you don't know why I'm angry*?'

'Actually, I didn't accuse you of treating me like a prostitute. I just said that if you paid for everything it would make me feel like a prostitute. That isn't the same thing.'

'Have you any idea how many women have wanted to hear me say the words I just said to you?'

'I'm sure lots of women would have been very flattered,' she mumbled, and he inhaled sharply.

'But you're not one of them?'

'No.' She swallowed. 'Unfortunately not.'

He ran a hand over his face, visibly struggling with his temper. 'What do I have to do? *What is it you want from me?* Tell me, because I'm damned if I know.'

'Nothing.' She almost choked on the word. 'That's the point. Our circumstances are just too far apart. I can't afford to live with you as your equal and I won't let you keep me.'

'Chantal—' His voice was tense. 'All around the world there are couples living together whose financial situation is not equal. Men go out to work, women raise children. In some families that situation is reversed, but one thing is sure—they don't all have financial equality.'

'Maybe not.'

'I can't believe you're saying no to me.'

She swallowed and looked out of the window. 'That's just because no one has ever said no to you before. You'll get over it. It will probably be character building.'

'My character is fully formed,' he muttered thickly. 'What I don't understand is *why* is this issue is so important to you.'

She stilled. 'It just is.'

'No.' He turned to face her, his tone was an angry growl. 'That isn't good enough. If I'm supposed to let you go, Chantal, then at least do me the courtesy of explaining *why*.'

She stayed silent, aware that he was almost boiling with impatience in the seat next to her.

'Chantal.' His tone was dark and threatening. 'I'm not letting you go unless—'

'My mother was a prostitute.'

She heard his sharply indrawn breath and turned to look at him. 'That's right.' She was surprised by how calm she sounded. 'That's who I am, Angelos. The daughter of a prostitute. Obviously getting pregnant with me was a career-limiting move, but she managed to get round that.'

'Chantal—'

She turned her head, unable to look at him. Humiliation threatened to crush her, but she forced herself to give him the details he needed to hear. 'You wanted the truth, and I'm telling you the truth just this once. After this don't ever ask me to talk about it again.' Why had she bothered saying that, when she knew that after this he wouldn't want to go anywhere near her? She knew full well that this was going to be the last conversation they ever had. 'At first we moved around a lot. I started a new school every term.'

'Look at me, Chantal.' He reached out and touched her arm, but she shrank away from him, her eyes still fixed in the middle distance.

'I found it hard to settle in.'

After a moment, he let his hand drop. 'I'm sure you did. I understand now why you found school difficult and couldn't wait to leave. Did they know about your mother?'

'Oh, yes.' She kept her tone light. 'No matter how hard I tried to keep it a secret, somehow someone always found out what my mother did. Obviously no one was allowed to be friends with me—no one wanted to be. And when I was on my own in the playground, or being tormented, I used to just escape in my head and pretend I was someone else. If I hated the situation I was in, I just imagined something different.'

There was a tense silence. 'You don't have to talk about this,' he breathed and she turned then and allowed herself to look at him. *For the last time.*

'I do have to talk about it. It's important that you understand who I am.'

His dark brows met in a sharp frown. 'This isn't about who you are.'

'Yes, it is. It's what shaped me. It's what made me who I am.'

And having to reveal herself to this man was the lowest point of her life. Hot tears of humiliation stung her eyes and for a moment she wondered whether she had what it took to carry on. And then she remembered how they'd reached this point. He thought he had feelings for her. *But he didn't know who she really was, did he?*

She blinked rapidly. 'When I was ten, my mother met a very rich man. He introduced her to another rich man, and pretty soon her entire clientele had changed. We went up in the world. I suppose you could call it a promotion. I was sent to a very elite boarding school, with my fees paid by one of her regulars.'

'The girls at the boarding school—'

'Did they know what my mother did? Oh, yes—' She gave a humourless laugh. 'Several of them had fathers who were my mother's clients—although I don't think any of them actually realised that.'

He rubbed his fingers over his forehead and muttered something in Greek. 'Now I understand why your schooldays were difficult.'

'Those girls stripped away what little confidence I had—' She swallowed. 'And I let them, because I suppose deep down I hated myself as much as they hated me. I was the daughter of a prostitute. Hardly something to boast about, was it? That's why I travelled. I always hoped I could leave it behind, but it never worked that way because it's part of who I am.' *And it always would be.*

'Do you still see your mother?'

Chantal shook her head. 'She was never interested in me. She only put me in that school because one of her clients thought she wasn't paying me enough attention. Anyway, I left at sixteen—' She gave a tiny shrug. 'I had no wish to stay there any longer than I had to.'

'Did the school do nothing about the fact you were bullied?'

'The school was horrified by the effect that having me as a pupil had on their reputation. They were delighted when I decided to leave.'

He was silent for a moment, his powerful body still. 'And that's why you're so determined never to take money from a man. Now I understand why you keep thrusting money at me.'

'I promised myself that I would never let a man keep me.' She looked at him, hanging onto her composure with difficulty. 'So now you understand. Will you explain to your father? And tell him why? I'd hate him to think less of me.' The tears were building, and this time she knew she wasn't going to be able to hold them back. In order to prove to him that their relationship would never work she'd lifted her protective shield and allowed him to see who she really was.

'Chantal—'

'Thanks, Angelos.' Choked by humiliation, she couldn't bear to hear what he had to say and so reached down and picked up her bag. 'You may be filthy rich and arrogant, but you never once made me feel small or insignificant. You're a pretty decent guy, really, but I promise not to ruin your reputation by telling anyone.' Without giving him time to reply, she opened the car door and stepped into the crazy Athens traffic.

Her vision was so severely blurred by tears that she narrowly missed being run over twice as she darted across the road. Horns blared, drivers shouted abuse in Greek, but she just kept running, banking on the fact that he wouldn't be able to follow her quickly.

She reached the other side and lost herself in a maze of side streets and then, finally, she stopped running and leaned against a wall.

She could hear shouts and the crashing of plates and cutlery from a nearby kitchen, a man yelling abuse from an apartment high up above her and the constant noise of traffic. And nearby she heard the sound of someone crying: muffled, heart-wrenching sobs, so pitiful and desolate that a few people paused and glanced with concern.

Only when she saw that they were looking at her did she realise that *she* was the one who was crying. And she sank to the ground and gave way to the emotion that had been building inside her.

CHAPTER TEN

IT WAS the last half-hour of her shift.

Chantal placed the drinks on the table and took out her notepad. 'Are you ready to order?'

'Can we have five minutes?' The group of American tourists were still huddled over the menu, arguing about the translation.

Chantal smiled at them and glanced around the café, checking that no one else was trying to attract her attention. Unable to help herself, her eyes slid to the road—but there was no sports car, no Greek billionaire—no one.

She tried to lift her flagging spirits.

What had she expected?

That he'd come after her?

How ridiculous was that? Why would he come after her when she'd spent so much time carefully explaining why she couldn't stay with him? And anyway he didn't know where she was.

He wouldn't know that she'd chosen to come back to Paris, would he? He'd assume that she'd moved on somewhere new, as she always had in the past. And she probably should have done exactly that.

But she just hadn't been able to bring herself to do it.

Paris was something that she'd shared with him. It was as if by being here she was holding on to a tiny part of him.

She didn't understand why there was some comfort in

knowing that he'd walked these streets and breathed this air, but
there was.

Not that it made any difference. Even if he did know where
she was, he wouldn't care.

He knew who she was now. No more hiding. No more pretending.

Trying to ignore the dull feeling of misery that had sat in her
insides for every moment of the last month, Chantal walked
briskly back to the American party and helped them with their
menu.

Her shift came to an end, and she made her way back to the
old house in which she rented a room. As usual the key refused
to turn in the lock, and it took a further five minutes of determined
coaxing before she was able to gain access to her property.

As she climbed the five flights of stairs to her tiny room, she
wondered what Angelos was doing.

Dining with a room full of diplomats?

Negotiating some mega-deal in New York?

Or lying by the pool discussing the money markets with his
father?

Infuriated by the lump in her throat, she pushed open the
door of her room and stopped dead.

The subject of her thoughts was sprawled on her sofa—six
foot two of powerful Greek male dominating the tiny room.

She blinked several times, wondering whether her vision was
playing tricks on her. Was the power of wishful thinking really
that strong?

'What are you—? How did you get in?'

'Your landlady let me in.' He glanced around him. 'I don't
know what she's charging you, but whatever it is you've been
robbed. This place isn't fit for human habitation.'

Stunned that he was there, and not understanding what could
possibly have brought him all this way, Chantal pushed the door
shut. 'What are you doing here?'

'Claiming what's mine.' His glance was unmistakably possessive and she felt her legs tremble.

'Angelos—'

'Start packing. I gave your landlady notice. You're going to
need something bigger than this.'

She dropped her bag on the floor. 'I can't afford anything
bigger.'

'Yes, you can.'

She closed her eyes. *Hadn't he listened to a word she'd said?*
Or had he just been stubborn? 'I've already told you I don't want
your money—'

'I'm not offering you my money.' His voice a soft drawl, he
rose to his feet. 'Sit down, Chantal.'

Her legs were shaking so badly that she plopped down onto
the nearest chair without argument, staring at the neat file he
dropped into her lap. 'What's this?'

'It's your business plan. Some of the figures may be a little
on the conservative side, but I've factored in reduced working
hours.'

She glanced up at him. 'Reduced working hours? I don't
know what you're talking about.'

He gave her a confident smile that was unashamedly masculine. 'You won't be designing clothes when we're in bed and
since we're going to be spending a significant proportion of our
time there the figures have been adjusted to give you a relatively
short working day. But the profit margins are incredible.'

'I *still* don't know what you're talking about.'

'I want us to be together, and since you won't agree to that
unless you're financially independent then the obvious solution
is to make you financially independent. Read the business plan.'

Dazed and confused, she opened the file on her lap and started
to read. *'Zouvelekis Couture?'*

'You already have at least twenty desperate customers waiting
for you to dress them for various important occasions, so read

fast,' he advised, a satisfied gleam in his eyes as he registered her astonishment. 'As I said, you can't work from this room.'

'You're suggesting I make dresses?'

'Don't misunderstand me,' he drawled. 'I don't care what you choose to do in life as long as it delivers an income which will allow you to transcend that major hang-up of yours.'

She flipped through the file. 'I couldn't possibly charge that much—'

'I knew you would say that, and I have already appointed someone qualified to deal with pricing issues.' He removed the file from her hand and pulled her to her feet. 'You can either take a salary and pay me in rolls of used notes at the end of every month, or alternatively your company can become part of Zouvelekis Industries. Whichever makes you feel more comfortable.'

She stood up. 'Angelos, I can't just—'

'*Don't* give me any more objections,' he warned. 'Because I have already spent hours crunching the numbers on this one and researching your potential market. As far as I'm concerned the problem is solved.'

It was difficult to breathe. 'You've spent hours on it?'

'Yes.'

'You did that for me?'

'No. I did it for *me*,' he murmured dryly. 'So that you can come and live with me.'

'You still want me to live with you?'

'It's hard to sustain a marriage when the two people aren't together.'

Her knees gave way and she plopped back down onto the chair. 'What did you just say?'

'What is the matter with you?' He looked at her with unconcealed impatience. 'You are repeating everything I say, not listening.'

'I'm just—I don't know what to say.'

'Then I'll do that talking. You owe me three euros.'

Her head was spinning. 'What for? Angelos, did you just say—?' But the words stuck in her mouth, because he was drawing something out of his pocket, something glittery and polished and— 'It's a ring.'

He dragged her back to her feet and hauled her against him. 'In between writing your business plan and researching the market for couture clothes, I found a ring. I bought you a rare pink diamond, originally purchased by a rich sheikh for his youngest wife. It was of unsurpassed beauty and great historical significance.'

She stared doubtfully at the cheap plastic ring that he still held in his hand. 'I think they saw you coming.'

He glanced down at the ring, as if he'd forgotten he was holding it. 'This isn't that ring. I suddenly realised that if I presented you with a rare pink diamond of unsurpassed beauty and great historical significance you'd only agree to accept it if I let you pay.'

'Oh.' Her heart performed several tiny jumps. 'You're starting to know me quite well—'

'So I bought you this instead.' He took her hand and slipped the ring on her finger. 'It's plastic and it cost three euros. If you want to reimburse me for it, that's fine. I don't care, as long as you agree to marry me.'

Her stomach dropped and her mouth fell open with disbelief. 'You want to marry me?'

'Why does that surprise you?'

'Well, because—' she licked her lips '—because I'm—'

'Good, kind, beautiful, generous, independent, modest, impossibly sexy—'

'Stop!' She cut him off with a bubble of nervous laughter. 'Angelos, *you can't marry me*!'

He pulled a face. 'Never say *can't* to me,' he advised silkily, running a gentle finger over her cheek. 'It's the one word guaranteed to send me into achievement overdrive.'

'*My mother was a prostitute.*'

'I don't care if your mother was a hippopotamus,' he drawled 'I'm not proposing to your mother. I'm proposing to you.'

She made a sound that was somewhere between a sob and a laugh. 'You can't do this. You're making the wrong decision—'

'*Wrong* is another word you should never say to me. My ego is far too fragile to accept it.' His eyes teased her but she was too shaken to respond.

'You'll regret it—I'll embarrass you—'

'You could never embarrass me. On the contrary, I'm immensely proud of you.'

'Your father—'

'My father insists on it.' He took her face in his hands, his eyes holding hers. 'You are an essential addition to the family. But there is something I want to know. That night of the ball, why did you tell my father that we were a couple?'

'Because it was what I wanted,' she said shyly. 'I was pretending.'

'Just like you used to pretend in the playground.' He gave a slow, satisfied nod, as if she'd given the answer he'd wanted and expected. 'It was only after you left that I worked that out and realised that you loved me.'

The fact that he knew how she felt left her feeling horribly vulnerable. She tried to pull away from him, but his hands held her firmly.

'You're not running away from me this time. You won't take anything material, and I understand that.' His voice was hoarse. 'That's why I'm not giving you an expensive ring. I won't give you a reason to refuse me.'

'Angelos—'

'Do you have any idea how I felt that night when you told me

ll those things about your mother and then just ran into the
niddle of the road? I thought you were going to be killed!'

'I felt so terrible—'

'I know you felt terrible, and I wanted to follow you and tell
ou that none of it mattered. But by the time I crossed the road
ou had vanished.'

'You abandoned your car in the middle of all that traffic?'

'Yes—and that required some fast talking with the police
vhen I eventually returned to it. *Where were you?* When I
ealized you must have had your passport on you, I had a team
f people at the airports and the ferry, but no one could find you.'

'Yes, well, I've always kept my passport with me at all
imes—I've travelled around so much it became an automatic
abit,' she explained. 'I worked in Athens for a few weeks until
'd made enough money to come here.'

'Why Paris?'

'Because—' She broke off, and he breathed out slowly and
gently rubbed her cheek with his thumb.

'Because this is where we first met? That is why I chose to
ook here.' He slid his arms around her and dragged her hard
gainst him. 'Promise me that you will never, *ever* run from me
gain.'

'We can't be together—' Her face was muffled against his
hest. 'Our circumstances are just too different.'

'Money is not the issue here. I'm not offering you money. I'm
ffering you the things that money can't buy—the things you've
ever had before like emotional support and my protection.'
His hold on her tightened. 'If someone so much as *looks* at you
he wrong way, or makes you feel inferior or awkward, I'll knock
hem flat.'

Unbelievably touched, she gave a stifled laugh. 'I've always
hought you had a dodgy temper.'

'I'm offering you my family, Chantal,' he said softly, relaxing
is hold so that he could look at her. 'My father's divorces ripped

us all apart—I think you know that. If I was harsh with you when we met, it's because I was determined not to let another woman trample over my family. But that was before I fell in love with you.'

It took her a moment to find her voice. 'You *love* me?'

'Yes. And until I met you I'd given up on ever loving a woman the way my father loved my mother.'

'Love?' She still couldn't believe she was hearing him correctly. 'You're offering me love?'

'What did you think? Why do you think I want us to be together?'

She blushed awkwardly. 'I suppose—sex?'

'You think a man would only ever be interested in you for sex. You are clearly unaware of the many qualities you possess,' he said softly, and then smiled. 'The fact that you're an incredibly exciting woman is a bonus.'

She was so overwhelmed she could hardly speak. 'Qualities? *Many* qualities? No one has ever said anything like that to me before.'

'Well, get used to it, because I'll be saying it all the time,' he drawled. 'I want a great deal more than sex from you, *agape mou*. I am a very ambitious man. I want *everything*. And I want to give you everything in return. In time I'm even hoping that you'll let me spoil you in a material way, but if your business takes off the way I know it will, you will be able to spoil yourself under my direction.'

'I can't believe you're saying this. I love you too,' she mumbled, burying her face in his chest. 'I really do. I think I loved you from the first moment I saw you.'

'I know you did.' He shrugged. 'How could you not?'

Half-laughing, half-crying, she tilted her head to look at him. 'Arrogant.'

'Confident.' Supremely sure of himself, he smiled down at her. 'So? Will you make my father a happy man and marry me?'

She gave a choked laugh of disbelief. 'You thought I was a gold-digger.'

'It was a natural assumption for a man in my position. You have to understand that my father's last two wives both fitted that description…' He hesitated. 'And I once had a similar experience myself.'

'You did?'

'I was just eighteen and I thought she cared about me.' He shrugged. 'Fortunately for me I discovered the truth about her before too much damage was done, but it was a lesson that I didn't forget.'

'You were hurt?'

'Honestly?' He gave a wry smile. 'My ego was more bruised than my heart, because I was forced to acknowledge that I wasn't all things to all women. But it did teach me to be wary.'

'I understand that. And I don't blame you for thinking that about me.'

'I did not think it for long. And my father *never* thought it. He loved you from that first moment.'

'At that ball in Paris—someone recognised me from my old boarding school. She came over, and I was so horrified that I couldn't speak. Your father rescued me and sent her packing. I couldn't believe he would do that for a stranger. I fell in love with him on sight. No one had ever done something like that for me before.' She smiled up at him. 'What do you think he will say when you tell him?'

'He will be delighted.' His arms tightened around her. 'It's just as well I saw you first, or I think he might have made you his fourth wife.'

'I love him.' Her smiled faded as she gazed into his breath-takingly handsome face. 'I kidded myself that I was only staying for your father's sake, but it wasn't true. I was staying because I couldn't bear to leave you.'

'And you're not going to leave me ever again.' He lowered his head and kissed her gently. 'I love you.'

'I can't believe you don't care who I am—'

'I *love* who you are. You are gentle and good and soon you will also be confident.'

She pulled a face. 'I can't imagine ever being confident.'

'With me loving you, how could you not be? We will work on it together.'

'*Zouvelekis Couture…*' She tilted her head to one side. 'You want my business to have your name?'

'Soon it will be *your* name too, and everyone will know that you are my wife.'

'Are you sure you want people to know?' She caught his look of exasperation and blushed. 'Sorry, sorry. It's just that I can't become confident overnight. You'll have to teach me how—just as you've taught me everything you know about sex.'

'Ah…' He gave a wicked smile and lowered his head to hers, his lips teasing the corner of her mouth. 'I haven't taught you *everything* I know about sex. There are definitely a few more things you need to learn.'

'Is that right?' Chantal wound her arms around his neck and smiled up at him. 'In that case, what are we waiting for?'

Queens of Romance

Bedding His Virgin Mistress
Ricardo Salvatore planned to take over Carly's company, so why not have her as well? But Ricardo was stunned when in the heat of passion he learned of Carly's innocence…

Expecting the Playboy's Heir
American billionaire and heir to an earldom, Silas Carter is one of the world's most eligible men. Beautiful Julia Fellowes is perfect wife material. And she's pregnant!

Blackmailing the Society Bride
When millionaire banker Marcus Canning decides it's time to get an heir, debt-ridden Lucy becomes a convenient wife. Their sexual chemistry is purely a bonus…

Available 5th September 2008

Collect all 10 superb books in the collection!